# EMBER

## THE COMPLETE SERIES

NEW YORK TIMES &
USA TODAY BESTSELLING AUTHOR
DEBORAH BLADON

# COPYRIGHT

First Original Edition, June 2015


ISBN-13: 978-1514637449
ISBN-10: 1514637448

Cover Design by Wolf & Eagle Media

This book is a work of fiction. Any resemblance to actual persons, living or dead, or actual events is entirely coincidental. Names, characters, businesses, organizations, places, events and situations either are the product of the author's imagination or are used factiously.

## *Also by Deborah Bladon*

*The Obsessed Series*
*The Exposed Series*
*The Pulse Series*
*The VAIN Series*
*The RUIN Series*
*IMPULSE*
*SOLO*
*The GONE Series*
*FUSE*
*The Trace Series*
*CHANCE*

# EMBER

## PART ONE

NEW YORK TIMES &
USA TODAY BESTSELLING AUTHOR
DEBORAH BLADON

# ONE

"If you're coming back to my place I need to buy some condoms."

The fork in my hand stops in mid-air. I don't look up. I can't. I've barely taken one bite of the roasted squash salad the waiter brought me not more than four minutes ago. This is New York City. This is the place where I thought I'd find the love of my life. What the hell was I thinking?

"You're up for coming back, right?"

My head darts up and I study him. This might actually be the first time I've seriously looked right at him. I'm on a blind date. Maybe the term itself holds more meaning than the literal. Obviously, I had no idea what Larry looked like before I walked through the doors of Axel NY a half hour ago. More than that, I couldn't have predicted that we'd be talking about sex before I'd finished my first glass of wine.

"I don't know you," I say bluntly. "Why would I go home with you?"

It's a question that borders heavily on rhetorical. I don't think that Larry's bright enough to weave those jumbled pieces of subtly together. He's an assistant to a paralegal. That says a lot about his drive in life considering he looks like he's in his mid-forties. He's also dying to be fucked. He's not shy about it at all.

"We're on a date, Bridget." The words linger there on his thin, smug lips. He doesn't add to them because why would he? Those words have clearly and succinctly spelled out every intention that he has. They aren't masked in anything but the truth. Larry wants his dick to see some action tonight and I'm apparently the main attraction in that circus.

"It's just a date," I explain. "I'd like to get to know you first."

"Why?" He pushes the food from his fork into his mouth and chews.

"I'm not interested in a quick fuck."

His unruly brow cocks. "I heard you were up for just about anything."

*Fuck you, Zoe Beck. Fuck you for whatever the hell you said to him when you arranged this date.*

"I have no idea what my friend told you about me," I pause while I contemplate how to put this delicately. I stare at him. The wayward piece of kale that is stuck between his front teeth is only adding to the allure that is Larry.

He rests his forearms on the table. The patch on the elbow of his inexpensive suit jacket brushes against the linen tablecloth. "This place isn't cheap. I brought you here because I thought you were a sure thing."

*A sure thing? A fucking sure thing?*

I wince at the words. "The only sure thing tonight is that you're going home alone."

It's obvious immediately that Larry is contemplating those words with all the grace of a pack of wild dogs. His hand slams heavily against the spotless white linen tablecloth. "I didn't buy you that expensive salad for nothing. The least you can do is blow me."

No, the least I can do is tell him to fuck right off. "I am not interested in you."

"I'm not interested in you either." He flings his napkin at me and it lands squarely in my squash salad. I was going to have another bite of that. "I like brunettes, not blondes."

Touché.

"I like men with hair."

Ouch. I can feel Larry's pain from across the table. Obviously no one, including all the brunettes he's been with, has pointed out the bad comb over that's happening on the top of his odd shaped head.

"We're leaving now."

I actually look to the right and the left to see who Larry is talking to. I'm gathering that he's still engaged in a conversation with me even though I'm trying desperately to ignore him. People are starting to stare and I have no aversion to a little extra attention, but tonight, I don't want to be the main attraction in Larry's sideshow.

"Get up." He grabs tightly to my bicep and yanks hard.

I cry out sharply. Considering the fact that most of my body is still stuck next to this table in a chair, my arm can't leave with Larry. "Let go of me."

"Is there a problem?" A deep, husky voice asks.

I turn towards it even though Larry is still trying to separate my arm from my shoulder to take as a consolation prize. I look up into the dark eyes of a brown haired man. He's staring down at me with a noticeable look of concern on his face.

"Hey," he calls across the table at Larry. "Enough. You're hurting her."

"Get lost." Larry loosens his grip only momentarily. "My girlfriend and I don't need your help."

*Wait. No. Hell no.*

"I'm not your girlfriend," I growl at him. "Let go of my arm already."

"You're coming with me." Larry pulls harder and I can't help but cry out in pain.

Within an instant my arm is free and the lapel of Larry's jacket is firmly entrenched in the fisted hands of the handsome man with the dark eyes.

"Are you okay?" He cocks a winged brow while he holds tight to Larry. "Did he hurt you?"

"I'm fine." My voice is quiet and small. Maybe I'm not as fine as I thought. I lean my hands on the table, suddenly feeling dizzy.

I hear movement behind me before I sense someone crouching next to me. "He's gone. Are you sure you're okay?"

I turn to the left and look into the same deep brown eyes. "I'm fine. He just shook me up."

"He may have torn something in your shoulder." He presses it lightly with his fingers. "I'd get it checked out if it's sore tomorrow."

"Are you a doctor?" I know he's probably on a date with someone. The dark suit he's wearing doesn't hide his muscular frame.

"No." A small grin pulls at the corner of his mouth. "I'm a firefighter. I'm Dane."

"Bridget Grant," I say with a wince as I try to move my arm to shake his hand.

"I'm taking you to the ER now." He pulls on the back of my chair. "Come with me."

I don't protest. Why would I? He's a fireman and he wants to rescue me. I may actually have to thank Zoe for this date, after all.

***

I had such high hopes before we arrived at the ER. Dane had wrapped his arm around me as he led me out of the restaurant to the street. At first I thought he was feeling the same attraction to me that I was obviously feeling towards him. I didn't hesitate to thank him over and over again for pulling me free from Larry's grasp.

He had hailed a taxi and as he sat next to me in the hurried ride over, he hadn't said a word. It was a direct and very awkward contrast to what I was doing. I'm not great with silence. I don't know if it stems from the fact that I'm an only child. We lived in rural Connecticut when I was growing up and my stuffed animals and dolls became my closest friends. They knew all my secrets and I counted on them to keep me company after school and on weekends. My mother worked during the day while my father tended to the household chores and yard work. Once my mother's car pulled into the driveway, he'd give her a quick kiss goodbye and head to his job as a bartender at a nightclub. I have only a few memories of the three of us together.

"The wait is close to four hours." I can hear the frustration in Dane's voice as approaches where I'm sitting in the very crowded waiting room.

It's already near ten, which means that I'll be lucky if I get back to my apartment before dawn. "I can just call a doctor in the morning. My friend, Vanessa, is a nurse. I'm sure she'll be able to point me to a clinic tomorrow to have my shoulder checked out."

"Your friend Vanessa is a nurse?" He grins for the first time since we left the restaurant. "My cousin is marrying a nurse named Vanessa."

I rest my hand in my lap trying to relieve the shooting pain that is radiating through my shoulder. "That's a weird coincidence. My friend actually works here. I should check if she's on duty."

"She's not." His mouth twists into a wider smile. "I asked at the desk. She has the night off."

"Your cousin is Garrett Ryan?" Pushing myself up I gaze across the room towards the nurses' station. "You're talking about Vanessa Meyer, right?"

"One in the same," he says as he points at my shoulder. "You're sure you want to leave that until tomorrow. I can wait around with you if you want."

It's an offer that's almost too tempting to refuse. As handsome as he is, I know that I pulled him away from something, or more than likely, a stunning someone. I've been left high and dry in the middle of a date by a man before so I know the humiliation that comes with that.

I hadn't wanted to stare, but when he was standing by the nurses' station a few minutes ago checking on the wait times, I'd seen him make a call on his smartphone. His brow had shifted just as his lips started moving. He lowered his head right then and within that motion I saw a flash of regret pour over his expression. It had to have been her. His instinctive need to rescue me had taken him away from someone in that restaurant.

"You should head back to Axel." I look over his shoulder, not wanting to make eye contact with him. I feel guilty that I want him to stay. "I'm sure your date is waiting for you."

"She's not." He turns his head towards me. "No one is waiting for me."

In the middle of this bustling hospital waiting room I can't tell if there's a subtle proposition woven into the words or not. "Do you want to take me home?"

His head lifts as he takes a second to rake his eyes over the tight black dress I'd somehow managed to fit myself into earlier. "I ended my relationship tonight. If I take you home, Bridget, I'll want to stay."

"You ended your relationship?" I try to swallow past the lump that has now formed in my throat. He's gorgeous, he's single and he's hurting. It's a trifecta of one night stand perfection.

He nods as he reaches past me to pick up my small clutch purse that had slipped onto the chair I was sitting in when I stood. "I could use a friend."

I could use a fuck so without another thought I let him take me by the hand and lead me out of the waiting room and into a night I have a feeling I'm never going to forget.

# TWO

I lusted too soon. When Dane said he needed a friend it wasn't code for *I want to fuck you into tomorrow*. Apparently, I'd crossed paths with that mythical creature that all single women in Manhattan have heard of but haven't seen. In fact, I don't think there's been a spotting in years. It's the highly desired, but virtually non-existent, nice guy and right now, I'm sitting at my kitchen table staring right at one in the form of Dane Beckett.

He had guided me through the door of my building and then into the elevator as if I was a wounded doe. As he pulled me into his side to shield my shoulder from the other occupants in the lift I'd felt the compassion in his touch. It's in his eyes too.

I'd asked him to unzip my dress as much to help me because my shoulder was still too tender to move, as it was a silent invitation. I could see our reflection in the hall mirror as he pulled slowly on the zipper and my overly active libido thought he might actually slide his hands beneath the fabric so he could cup my breasts. He'd bent his chin down and although I could only see his profile in the mirror, I knew he was staring at my bare skin.

It's near ten minutes later now and just as I walked back into the kitchen after changing into sweatpants and a t-shirt, he'd stood to introduce himself. He'd held out his hand in a gallant gesture that spoke of good manners and a respect for women that is rare in the circles I travel in. He's a gentleman and as we sit and sip from our mugs of hot coffee, I feel the weight of a dozen questions bearing down on me.

"That guy that you were having dinner with said you were his girlfriend. Is that true?" he asks just as I'm about to talk about the food at the restaurant. In my over tired mind it's the perfect segue to get him to open up about the woman he dumped tonight. I'm typically not the type to care about other people's relationships unless they are six foot tall firemen who look irresistible in a well-tailored suit and the beginnings of a five o'clock shadow covering their rugged jawline.

"Larry?" I say before I realize that I'm not even sure that's his name. It may have been Terry or Garry. No, it was Larry. "I have a friend who interns at a law office. Larry works there too. She set us up."

"She's a friend? I'd hate to see who your enemies would set you up with."

Zoe's going to hate seeing me when I get my hands on her tomorrow. Unless she's never met Larry in the sweaty flesh there's no logical explanation for why she thought I'd find him attractive. She knows my type. Larry is about as far from that as a man can get. Dane, on the other hand…

"So you're not seeing anyone?"

I look away. He's not tempering anything. The man is on a serious mission to find out my dating status. At least that's the way I'm interpreting it. I've been misreading his cues all night though so in reality he's probably asking if I have a significant other because he thinks I'm in mortal danger living in this part of the city alone. He may be right but I have a bunch of self defense moves my father taught me to fall back on.

"I'm not seeing anyone," I say it clearly knowing that now is my prime chance to turn the tables on him. "You said earlier you broke up with your girlfriend tonight."

"It's over," he grumbles. Tension grips his shoulders. He leans back in the chair. "We were celebrating something. I just looked up at her and realized I wanted out."

Dumping someone in the middle of a celebratory dinner doesn't align with the person who has tended to me for the past few hours. "That must not have been easy."

"It was necessary." His dark eyes settle on my face. "It hasn't worked for a while. Why waste time with something you know isn't right for you?"

It's a rhetorical question that I'm tempted to answer. I've been in the shoes of the woman he broke up with tonight. I've tried holding onto a relationship I knew wasn't working because I didn't want my investment to be all for nothing. That was years ago though. It's different now. I have fun. I don't plan ahead and I don't worry for a second about whether a guy I'm with has long term potential.

"I completely agree." I trace my fingers over the rim of the mug. "I don't hang around if it's not working for me. After all, there are a lot of single people in the city."

"New York does have a lot to offer." He straightens in his chair. "You never know what's waiting for you at any given moment."

*My bed is waiting for us and the box of condoms I keep in the nightstand right next to it.*

"The possibilities are endless if you're open to them."

"I'm definitely open to them, Bridget." He pushes the mug away before rising from the chair. "Are you free tomorrow night?"

"I have to work until midnight," I begin as I look up at him. "I'm free on Friday."

"My birthday is today." He steps back from the table. "We'll celebrate it after midnight tomorrow."

"Happy Birthday." My hands fist in my lap. It's his birthday? How is it his birthday today? "You broke up with your girlfriend on your birthday?"

He studies me. "It's a new year for me. There's no better time to start fresh. What time will you be back here tomorrow night?"

"Around one," I say without any thought. "How do you want to celebrate?"

"Naked."

There's no hidden innuendo in that word at all. I sit frozen in my chair as he glances down at his smartphone, buttons his suit jacket and walks out of my apartment without a backward glance or another word.

# THREE

"I haven't met him yet." Vanessa pushes her fingers into my shoulder. "Garrett talks about him sometimes. I think he's a fireman."

"He told me that." I wince when her index finger drives into the tender spot near my shoulder blade. "That's it right there. It hurts like hell."

She rubs it gently. "He didn't do any permanent damage. I mean, I don't think he did. If it still hurts in a couple of days, stop by the hospital when I'm working and I'll get you into see one of the attending physicians."

I'm not sure if she has enough influence to help me skip the always endless line at the ER, but I'm grateful for the offer. "I'll keep an eye on it. I have to work tonight, so I'm hoping it's going to hold up through that."

"Carry the tray with your left hand if you can." She rounds me before dropping herself onto the couch a foot away from where I'm sitting. "If you put some heat on it, that will help loosen the muscles too."

I nod as I rub my shoulder. "Zoe's going to pay for setting me up with Larry."

"Larry?" She turns to the side, bending her leg at the knee so she can rest it between us. "Larry is the caveman who wanted to drag you into his bed?"

I visibly recoil at the mention of Larry and a bed in the same sentence. "I can't imagine what would have happened to me if Dane wouldn't have stepped in."

"You would have kicked Larry in the groin and shown him why he can't mess with you."

She's absolutely right. If Dane Beckett wouldn't have thrown himself into the skirmish between me and my date from hell, I would have taken matters into my own hands, or I would have put my knee into action. I can protect myself. I always have but having a man defend my honor was something I wasn't going to turn down.

"I'm going to steer clear of Zoe's matchmaking services from now on." I run the tip of my finger over the seam on the leg of my jeans. "She thinks she knows what's best for me but she doesn't always."

"Is that why you haven't shown her your drawings?" She leans her head into the soft leather of the couch. "I thought you were going to tell her about them so she could show them to Brighton."

Showing my pencil drawings to one of the world's most respected artists, Brighton Beck, may seem logical to Vanessa, but it's a terrifying proposition to me. I've shared my sketchbook with a handful of people, Vanessa included. Each of them has told me that they see lifelike emotion and beauty within the portraits that I sketch. I see my own vulnerability and weakness. I'm not at a point emotionally where I can hand them over to Zoe or Beck. It would mean exposing my inner self in a way that I'm not ready for yet because of the risk that's involved.

"I'll show her one day."

"They're going to be blown away when they see them, Bridget." She quiets for no more than a few seconds. "I'm in awe of your talent. Those drawings are breathtaking."

I came to her apartment with the intention of learning more about Dane, but talking about him involves a risk too. If she reaches out to him and says anything about me, it will spoil the uncomplicated attraction that is brewing between us. I'm not willing to mess with that so I change the subject to something I know she'll jump all over.

"How are you making out with your wedding plans? Do you need my help?"

Her eyebrows pop to life as her entire expression shifts. "Now that you mention it, there are a few things I could use help with."

***

"You're saying that a stranger is going to come over to your apartment tonight to fuck you?"

It sounds even hotter hearing it out loud.

"He's not a stranger." I place a glass of white wine on the small, circular table in front of Zoe. "Vanessa knows him."

"How well?" She takes a small sip of the wine before she pulls her face into a tight scowl. "This tastes strong."

"It's white wine." I slide my index finger and thumb along the stem of the glass. "I think you can handle it."

"I can," she says defiantly. Zoe Beck has been on a personal crusade the past few months to prove to no one but herself, that she's still capable of being a bad ass. It all started when she had her son, Vane. She felt herself losing touch with her friends, so she's made an extra strong effort to keep those connections alive. That's the only reason why she comes down here to Easton Pub every Tuesday, while I'm working, and orders a white wine.

We were roommates and co-workers before she met her husband, Brighton Beck. Once she moved in with him, everything changed. It's been inspiring watching her dreams coming true and it's been comforting having her friendship to rely on.

"He's a fireman, Zoe." I perch myself on the stool next to her. "He saved me from that lunatic Larry that you set me up with. That guy has serious issues."

"The fireman has serious issues?"

I throw my head back in feigned frustration. "Larry has issues. Why the hell did you set me up with him, Zoe? We have nothing in common and I'm pretty sure he is old enough to be my dad."

"He's not old enough to be your dad." She takes another sip of the wine. "You're twenty-three. He'd have to be at least in his early forties to be your dad, so I don't…wait…how old do you think he is?"

"Too old for me." My gaze moves to where my boss Elliott is standing by the bar. "He talked about buying condoms when I was trying to eat my salad."

"Elliott is looking over here." Zoe raises her hand to point in his direction unnecessarily. "Have you ever thought about giving it another try with him?"

I have. It's always when I'm feeling lost and alone or when I'm craving the touch of a man who knows what he's doing in bed. Elliott and I dated briefly right after I landed my job at the pub as a server. He was sweet, intense and went out of his way to make certain I was always satisfied sexually. He should be perfect for me but the pull towards him has never been strong enough to warrant cutting off the potential that exists out there. We've somehow managed to navigate the murky waters of our mutual break up to remain good friends and co-workers.

"Elliott and I are over." I slide off the stool. "I have to get back to work. I'll stop by in fifteen minutes to see if you want a refill."

She bows her head as a wide smile takes over her mouth. "You know I won't even finish this glass. Who am I kidding?"

"No one, Zoe." I wrap my arm around her shoulder to give her a half hug. "I won't tell anyone though. You're still a party girl to me."

"I'm not a party girl." She pauses, lifting her chin up. "You're the party girl. You're going to fuck a man you barely know. I've never done that in my life. You need to be careful."

I smile softly as I listen to her. I know I'm his rebound. I know how emotionally dangerous it is to crawl into bed with someone you barely know. I get all that but I'm aware enough to see this for what it is. He's hurting, I'm available and some really mind blowing sex can't hurt if I keep everything in perspective.

# FOUR

Dane's lips are soft, supple and as soon as he walks into my apartment and shuts the door behind him, they're on mine. His tongue slides out of his mouth and pulls at my lips, coaxing me to open my mouth to let him in. I do, just as his hands wrap around my waist before he pushes my back into the door.

"You live here alone don't you?"

They're words that should scare a single woman living in a less-than-secure building in New York City, but he's not asking so he can murder me in some ceremonial ritual. I know that. I sense it in his kiss and in the way his hands are sliding down my back towards my jean covered ass.

"I live alone," I whisper against his lips. "There's no one here but us."

His hands move to the bottom of the black tank top I'm wearing that is emblazoned with the Easton Pub logo. He pulls it over my head with ease and confidence before his gaze falls to my bra.

"I knew your body would be beautiful." He traces his index finger over the edge of the lace of my bra. "I could tell when you walked into the restaurant last night."

I part my lips to say something but my voice is stolen by the touch of his lips against my nipple. He tugs at the swollen bud through the black sheer lace. I cup my hand around the back of his head, guiding him closer to me, wanting him to pull it between his teeth so he can gift me with the rough burst of pleasure that comes from a touch of pain.

"I wanted to fuck you the minute I saw you."

My breath catches at the raw intensity of his words. I let him in to my apartment because I wanted this. My better judgment had pulled at the corner of my good sense when I was riding the subway home from the pub. I've slept with men I've just met in the past. It happened twice and both times it was because I was feeling a desperate need to indulge in the kind of dangerous pleasure that comes from knowing you're taking something that you'll never have again.

This time is different. Just the taste of his lips has created a craving within me that I know will be insatiable. The fact that I only know spotted details about who he is adds to the allure. I want him in a way that transcends logic and reason. My body is dictating every move I make and I have no intention of getting in its way.

I whimper softly when he reaches behind me and unclasps my bra with just two fingers. He pulls it free. The cool air in the room races over my bare flesh and I instinctively pull my hands up to cover myself. He catches them mid-air and holds them in his.

"Take me to your bed." His deep voice is edged with something. Lust, want, or it might be desperation. I can't tell and I don't care. Tonight this is purely about the pleasure we can take from each other. Nothing else matters.

***

"You're so wet and swollen, Bridget." His long fingers slowly run over my folds. "I can't wait to be inside of you."

I lean my hands back on the bed. He'd set me on the edge after pulling off my jeans and panties. He'd rid himself of his own clothes and as he did, I'd unabashedly stared at his body. It's rock hard. I've seen men who work out before, but Dane's body is a testament to strong will and commitment. He's as beautiful naked as anyone I've ever seen and right now, he's kneeling in front of me, his lips just mere inches away from my core.

"There are condoms in my nightstand." I jerk my chin towards the head of the bed to where the weathered wooden nightstand sits. "Put one on."

"You're in such a hurry." His lips curve around my left nipple before he sucks it into his mouth briefly to pull it between his teeth. "I'm not."

I sense the calmness in his voice that my entire body is lacking right now. Each time his fingers lightly graze my clit, my ass shifts slightly. I'm close to coming already and I know it's not just from the touch of his hand. I seriously want this man.

His hand leaves my core and I feel so bereft from the loss of his touch that I whimper aloud. His eyes dart up to my face. "I've never been with a woman with such a beautiful body."

They may be empty words of desire but that's not how I absorb them. I want him to view me as special. I want him to take something more than a fleeting post-orgasm high when he walks out of my apartment tonight. "You're beautiful too."

"I've never been called that before." He lowers his head briefly to glide his tongue over my smooth cleft.

I moan because trying to hold in the basic want I feel to have him can't be quelled. "That feels so good."

"I'm going to lick and suck you, Bridget." He licks me again, this time stopping to tongue my clit for no more than two beats of my racing heart. "You're going to suck my cock and then we're going to fuck."

It's all right there. His bluntness only makes me that much more aroused. I inch my ass forward on the bed, wanting him to claim my clit again. I'm shaking from the torture of being this close to an orgasm. My labored breathing is a plea for him to get me off.

He settles himself on his knees, pulls my legs over his shoulders and finally gives me everything I want and need.

# FIVE

"Sit on my lap."

I turn towards where he's sitting in a beige armchair in the corner of my bedroom. It's been hours since he ate me to two exquisite orgasms. I'd reached forward once he stood to take him into my mouth, but he'd pushed me onto my back, sheathed his thick cock in a condom and took me without any hesitation. I'd cried out when he fucked me hard. He didn't stop when I came. He didn't slow until he threw his head back, called out my name and came with a series of deep plunges.

His large hand is stroking his cock. He'd pulled on another condom when I went to the kitchen to get a glass of water and to catch my breath.

I walk across the room before I reach forward to grab his shoulders so I can lower myself onto his thighs. My hand skims over the cursive tattoo that covers the right side of his chest. I study the lettering but it's a language that is foreign and unfamiliar to me. "What does this say?"

His eyes dart down to where my hand covers his skin. "It's something my mother used to say to me."

The offer ends there. I don't push for more because this isn't about shared experiences or thoughtful memories of the people we care about. This is about sex. It's about escape, want and the need to feel something temporarily.

I slide my hand lower, circling it around the hard root. I want to feel him inside of me again. Soon dawn will break and he'll pull his jeans and sweater back on and disappear through my apartment door into the churning crowds that border the streets on any given morning. I'll never see him again and this night will be the only remembrance I have of this man's unforgettable touch.

His right hand jumps to my breast. He kneads the flesh in his hand, pulling on my tender nipple. "Slide your soft pussy over me."

I part my lips slightly with the hope that I'll be able to draw some much needed breath into my lungs. I inch forward, positioning myself so that the tip of the wide crown parts my outer folds.

"Jesus." His hands grip tightly to my hips. "This is way too fucking good."

I stare at his face as his head falls back into the chair. I pivot my hips, lean forward and lower myself down onto his cock.

He groans loudly, the sound of it reverberating through his chest. I pull back, rest my hands on his muscular thighs and slam myself back down onto his cock over and over again while he pumps his hips up with each stroke.

I come so hard that tears sting the edge of my eyes and just as he's about to release, his fingers circle my chin, his lips touch mine and he groans into our kiss.

***

"I start work in twenty minutes. I need to go." He's pulled the wrinkled sweater he threw on the floor back over his head. He rakes his hand through his hair although it does little to soften the disheveled mess it's become from my fingers. "What are you doing today?"

I tug on the bottom hem of the t-shirt I'd found at the foot of my bed. I'd felt so exposed and vulnerable after he'd kissed me for what felt like hours after we both came. His lips had trailed over mine, before they settled on my neck. He'd stayed there, clinging tightly to my body until his breathing leveled.

"I have to go to work tonight," I offer quietly. "I work almost every night."

"What do you do during the day?" He wipes two fingers across his lips as he briefly closes his eyes. "I'm going to smell you on me all day, Bridget."

My emotions stumble briefly. "I draw mostly. I go to Central Park and draw."

"As in pictures of trees?" He adjusts the leg of his jeans before pushing his feet back into the black loafers he kicked off when he came into my bedroom.

"No." I scratch the edge of my ear. I don't tell people about my art but I'm never going to see him again so there's no harm in revealing that part of me. "I do pencil drawings. I study people and then I draw them."

"You're an artist?" His mouth curves as his gaze flicks across the room. "I don't see any of them. Why aren't they hung on the walls?"

My confidence, or maybe it's my lack of confidence, keeps them hidden in a cardboard box under my bed. I rarely look at one once it's complete. I cover them with tissue paper, place them carefully in the box and slide it into the past, under my bed. "I'm a server. I'm not an artist."

"If you spend your days in the park drawing portraits of people you're an artist, Bridget." There's a pause before he continues. "You must be really talented."

My grin is genuine. I want to say something that will impact him enough that when he thinks back on this night, he'll remember me with a fondness that is rare. I just stand there staring into his deep brown eyes, marveling at how kind he was two nights ago when he took me to the hospital and how unrestricted his passion was last night.

"I need to go." He fumbles with his smartphone. "If I don't leave right now I'll be late."

The moment to capture something within him is gone. All that is left is the motion of following him to the door; looking at his face one last time and watching him walk away.

# SIX

"At least that strange man you let into your apartment last night didn't kidnap you." Zoe gently places Vane down in his crib. "If your mother knew that you were having sex with a man you don't know, Bridget, she'd flip out."

I've gotten used to Zoe's new motherly take on the world. If I meet her for lunch and I order a burger and fries, I know I'm going to hear about the dangers of eating too much fast food. If I show up at her apartment without a sweater on a chilly day, I'm going to be wearing one of her coats on my way home. It may be frustrating at times, but it's also endearing. She loves taking care of the people who matter to her and since I'm part of that cluster, I've learned to see the silver lining. I have a friend who loves me.

"I told you that Vanessa knows him." I skim my fingers over the baby's forehead. "He's Garrett's cousin."

"Wait. You didn't tell me that. I didn't know he was related to Vanessa."

I lean my hip against the side of the crib. "They're not related yet and she hasn't even met him."

"That's just semantics." She tucks her hair behind her ear. "If he's related to Garrett he has to be a good guy. Are you going to see him again?"

I want to. I've thought about him since he left my apartment early this morning. Since then I've gone to Central Park and sketched the face of a woman, who I guessed was a nanny, as she watched her young charges while they played near a fountain. The smile on her face didn't have a foundation in truth. She was sad. It was as if she was missing something that couldn't be replaced by a secure job and a day filled with the raucous laughter of pre-schoolers. She'd left something behind when she came to this country or maybe someone left her and all she wants is to escape from that pain.

Once I finished the last stroke of her eyebrow, I'd slid my pencil into my bag, tucked my sketch book under my arm and I'd gone to sit in front of the fire station down the block from my apartment. I'd watched the men and women who work there as they milled about inside of the large space. They'd all come outside when a man in a wheelchair and his wife passed by. The greetings were friendly and as they took the couple inside, I studied each face hoping to see Dane. I knew it was a twist of fate that wouldn't happen, but I'd wished briefly that serendipity would step in.

I'd gone home then to rest and as I lay in my bed, I caught the scent of his skin on my sheets. I closed my eyes, drifting off to the tortured reminders of his tongue on my core and his hands pulling me closer to him.

"Bridget." Zoe taps her finger on my shoulder. "Do you want something to eat before you go to work?"

I glance down at the tank top and jeans I'd put on after I'd showered. Zoe had texted me, telling me she wanted to see me before work so I'd left early, took the subway to her place and hoped that she'd be able to take my mind off of Dane.

"I ate some leftovers before I left home," I half-lie. I'd searched my kitchen for anything edible and had come up with some Italian I'd ordered in three nights ago. Once I plated it, I realized it was about as appetizing as the container it had sat in so I'd thrown it in the trash. I'll grab something at the pub on my break.

"Have you found a new roommate yet?"

I know she's only asking out of a sense of guilt. Zoe had left me without a roommate when she moved in with her boyfriend, now husband, Beck. I'm making just enough at the pub to cover the rent mainly because the tips are stellar. It's a strain on my savings account though so I'm still searching for someone I can live with who will have the rent in on time. I've gone through three roommates since she left. None of them lasted more than a month or two.

'"Not yet." I shrug my shoulder. "I'm thinking about moving out. I can probably find someone looking for a roommate who has a better apartment than I do."

"When is your lease up?" She yanks on the top of the light blue blanket she put over Vane. The gentle sound of his breathing fills the quiet spaces in our conversation.

"In two months. I don't think I'll renew."

"You can move in with Beck and me. I'll put you on diaper duty." She winks to show she's teasing me.

"I'll find a new place." My gaze sweeps the room and settles on the silver clock that hangs on the wall opposite the crib. "I'm going to take off. I need to check out my schedule for next week before my shift."

"Can we do lunch on Friday? I miss hanging out."

"Lunch on Friday," I parrot back as I take one last look at Vane. "Text me the details. I'll be there."

# SEVEN

"The bar closes in ten minutes. Does that mean you'll be done?"

It's him. I've only heard his voice a few times but the raspy tone of it touches me in a way that I can't explain.

I look to the right to where he's standing. His hands are shoved in the pockets of his jeans, his torso covered by a bulky black sweater and his dark eyes are peering at me beneath the brim of a baseball cap.

"Dane," I say his name just to hear it from my lips. It contains all the uncontainable desire it did when he first pushed his lips into mine last night. "What are you doing here? How did you know I worked here?"

His index finger lightly grazes over the front of my breast, stopping to point at the logo. "I saw this last night."

I look down to where his finger is settled over my now hard nipple. I dart my tongue over my lips before I speak. "I didn't think I'd see you again."

His hand moves down to my waist as he flashes me a brilliant smile. "Am I just a one night stand to you, Bridget?"

I squeeze my eyes shut as I try and adjust to the fact that he's not only standing in front of me, he's asking for more. It may not be direct, but it's there woven within the tone of the question. I look up into his face. "I didn't say that. I assumed you needed someone to…"

He leans forward so far that I'm certain that his lush lips are going to glide over mine but he stops just short of touching me. "You assumed I needed someone to fuck away the memory of my ex."

It's not a question. It's a statement and if I'm being honest, it's the truth. I did think that. "Break ups can be hard."

"The second I tasted your sweet pussy I forgot about her," he hisses the words into my ear. "I came back for more."

I swallow hard. This is exactly what I've thought about all day. I wanted this and yet now, that it's happening I feel the earth shifting beneath my feet. This man has the capacity to unravel me and even though my mind is telling me to stop and think, my body can't resist the promise of his words and his touch.

***

"Suck it, Bridget," he says the words through labored breaths. "Not too fast. I don't want to come yet."

I'd said the same words to him when we first arrived back at my apartment and he undressed me in a heated rush. He'd pulled me onto the cold hardwood floor just inside the doorway, setting me atop his face as I rode him to an intense climax. I'd fallen forward, desperate in my need to recover from the orgasm as much as to retreat momentarily from his desire for me. It was raw and unyielding.

Now, he's standing above me, his feet a hips' length apart as he fucks my mouth slowly, leaning his ass into the wall behind him.

I moan around the thick root as I pump the base with my hand. He's thicker than any other man I've taken down my throat. I adjust my knees, hoping that my stance will give me more leverage.

He doesn't stop his languid, slow strokes. His cock glides between my lips and over my tongue with each pulse. "I knew you'd suck me like this. I knew you'd take it all."

I want to take it all. I push forward, wanting him to guide it in carefully but his primal need for release takes over and his hands drop to my head. He pushes the wide crest deeper down my throat. I gag momentarily which only excites him more. I feel him widen and swell in my mouth.

"You want to swallow it don't you?"

I look up into his face. I nod slowly knowing that I must look greedy and shameless but I don't care. I want him to mark me. I want his release to cover me. I want it in me and just as I feel his body tense, I pull the head to my lips, close my eyes and moan when he comes all over my tongue.

# EIGHT

"Show me your drawings." His hand cups my breast from behind.

I must have drifted off briefly after he'd come in my mouth. We're twisted together on the couch in my living room. The white blanket from my bed is covering us. He had to have gotten up to get that. It's a gesture that speaks of quiet consideration. It's a brief glimpse into the handsome stranger I first met a few nights ago at the restaurant.

"I don't show them to people," I begin before I realize how it sounds. "I've only shown them to a few people."

His hand tugs me tighter into his chest and stomach. I can feel his semi erect cock resting against my thigh. It's too comfortable a position for two people who met only days ago yet it feels like I was made to fit within the crux of his arm and within the curve of his stomach like this.

"How long have you been drawing for?"

No one I've ever known has asked me that question. It began when I young enough to hold a crayon in my fingers and pull the colors across the easel that my parents bought for my fifth birthday. I'd position my dolls in a row on my bed and draw each in the way that I'd see them. My mother would take the colorful pages and tack them to the refrigerator with magnets. I'd study those drawings and critique the lines and shapes, eventually pulling them down to throw them in the trash.

As I got older, I graduated to sketch pads and pencils I'd purchase at the art store in Greenwich with the money I'd make babysitting. I started to draw the people I knew and eventually that shifted to classmates and boys that seemed enchanting in high school.

I wanted to go to college to study art but that was a foolish approach to life they told me. My parents had tucked every spare penny they had away into my college fund. I was accepted to a community college in Rhode Island which meant an escape from home but not from the future they planned for me. I got my degree in sociology because they saw the promise of a career in social work for me. They saw my compassion towards others as a means to a secure financial future for me even though my heart only speaks through my art.

I moved to Manhattan right after graduation under the guise that I'd find a job here but when I went into Easton Pub to have a drink that first night, the manager handed me an apron, a schedule and a way to fund my love for drawing through a hefty pocket filled with tips each night. I've never looked back, or forward.

My parents have stopped asking about a job with the city or the state. They've stopped hoping that I'll use my education to change the world. The disappointment is there in every conversation we have and it suffocates me when I go home to visit. I was their one chance at making a difference, and I let them down.

"When did you start drawing, Bridget?" he repeats the question quietly.

"I was a child." I look at his arm as I answer. There's a small scar on his wrist. It's not large enough to notice in passing, but it's there marring his skin in a way that makes him even that much more mysterious. "Did you get this at work?"

He leans forward, his arms circling me even tighter. "I did. It was years ago."

"What happened?" I ask because I'm interested in his job but more than that I'm grateful for the reprieve from talking about myself. "Were you hurt?"

"Not badly." His breath whispers over my shoulder. "My wrist was broken. I had surgery."

"Not badly?" I look back at him. "I've never had a broken bone. I think that qualifies as being hurt."

"It comes with the job," he says as he feathers his lips over the sensitive skin of my neck. "Turn over so I can look at you."

I cling to his hand as I shift my body on the narrow couch so I'm facing him directly. He rests his cheek on his bicep. "Your eyes are really beautiful. They're such a pale blue."

I've always loved the color of my eyes. They're light blue, soft and expressive. I stare at his face, soaking in the rich masculine lines. His nose is strong and lean. His eyebrows are dark and full. There's a pain behind his eyes that I can only assume is connected to his break up but asking will only bring it all to the surface. "Did you always want to be a fireman?"

"No." He shakes his head slightly. "I wanted to be a fire truck when I was a kid."

I laugh as his gaze holds mine. "You outgrew that dream, did you?"

"I ride on a fire truck." His hand slides up my arm. "It's the second best thing."

I nuzzle in closer to him, inhaling the heady scent of the skin on his neck. I want this moment to last. I want this comfortable feeling to take us from these moments post intimacy into the outside world. Logically I know I'm his rebound and once he's pasted his heart back together, he'll move on but for now, being in his arms is the only place I want to be.

***

"If you say something to me… please say something…it would help," I stammer as I shift my bare feet over the cool floor.

He moves his lips but the only thing that escapes them is a quiet puff of air. I watch as he pivots his body forward, his head bowing down towards the bed.

"I know they're not gallery quality." My stomach knots with apprehension.

When he followed me into the bedroom, I hadn't hesitated before I pulled the large cardboard box out from under my bed. He had bent over to pick it up to place it on the sheets. When I removed the lid, his eyes had widened just as his hand jumped up to cover his mouth. He's looked at four, maybe five, of the drawings now and the only response I've gotten has been silence.

"You drew these, Bridget?"

I cover my lips briefly with my hand. "Yes. I drew all of those. They were all at different times, but they're all by me."

"How old are you?" His eyes flick over my face.

I wrap the blanket from my bed tighter around my shoulders. He'd gently put it around me before we left the living room. He's still nude and that only adds to my failure to focus and absorb what he's saying to me.

"How old am I?" I repeat back wanting to make certain that I didn't misinterpret his question. It would be understandable given the fact that I'm standing in a room with a beautiful naked man who is staring at my drawings.

"Yes. I want to know how old you are."

"I'm twenty-three."

"How can you be twenty-three and draw like this?" He gestures towards the box. "How are you not famous?"

"Famous?" I smile at the suggestion. "What do you mean?"

He shifts so he's on his knees. "I go to galleries. I've been to every museum in the city. These belong there."

I look down at my drawings. "No. They're good but they're not like that. I do them because I like to draw."

He picks up one and holds it towards the dim light that the lamp on my bedside table is throwing off. He studies it, twisting it slightly in his hand. "I can feel who this woman is by looking at this. I can sense the heartache that she feels. I see it. It's right there, Bridget."

My eyes fall from his face to his drawing. "I saw her outside a floral shop on the Upper East Side. She was sitting on a bench there and I drew her."

"She's in pain. Look at her hands. See how they're fisted together."

I take a step closer to the bed to study the drawing. "I think she lost someone. I think she was there at the shop buying flowers for a service or a wake. I felt that when I looked at her."

"You can't hide these in your room." He slides to the edge of the bed and onto his feet. "You need to show these to people."

I let the blanket fall from my shoulders as I push the drawings back into the box. "No. It's not the right time yet. I'm not ready for that."

"You're not ready." He scrubs the back of his neck with his hand. "Why aren't you ready?"

I tug at the edge of the box gently. "I don't know."

"You're hiding your talent away from everyone." His tone is warm. "The world outside of your apartment needs to see these."

# NINE

I've never been to a fire station before. Technically I'm not in one now. I'm across the street, sitting on the edge of a fountain, staring at the place where Dane works.

It's been two days since he left my apartment after I showed him my drawings. He'd insisted on taking my number. I hadn't hesitated because a connection that transcends my bedroom in the middle of the night is what I've wanted. I know that what I share with him is fleeting and not based in anything beyond great sex, but for now, I'm willing to ride the wave to see where it's heading.

He walks through the doors and lifts his hand towards me. My breath catches. I might have thought he was irresistible that first night in the restaurant when I saw his body covered in a suit, but today, watching him walk towards me wearing a dark polo shirt, navy pants and a fleece pullover resting over his forearm, I feel something else. I spot the New York Fire Department logo on his chest before I pull my gaze to his face.

"You came." The words leave his lips the moment he reaches the spot where I'm sitting. "I didn't know if you'd come."

My head tilts to the side, as I look at him in the bright light of day. It's not that he looks remarkably different. His hair is combed and his face shaven, but the essence of the man who has given me so much pleasure is right there, staring back at me. "You asked me to come."

He had. He'd sent me a text message this morning asking if I'd meet him for an early dinner. I had wanted to type back a response immediately but instead I had laid in my bed basking in the knowledge that my one night stand has now pushed itself into a week.

"There's a diner around the corner." He nods to the left. "We can grab something there before you have to go to work."

I nod, not knowing exactly what to say. I've never fucked a man, and then had dinner with him. It's always been the other way around.

"Come with me, Bridget." His hand falls to the small of my back and I let him guide me through the busy pedestrian traffic to what I hope is the first of many dates.

***

"Her name is Maisy." He tosses that out into our corner of the universe before he takes a large bite of the turkey sandwich he ordered when we sat down. I hadn't asked about her. Hell, I was talking about the thunderstorm that had filled the skies with brilliant flashes of lightening last night. Her name came out of left field to smack me right across the side of my face.

I don't need to ask who Maisy is. I've wondered about her name since he told me at the hospital that he'd broken up with his girlfriend. Maisy. I repeat it back in my mind. It's adorable. She's likely adorable.

"That's the girl you dumped?" I ask for clarification. I don't know why I need it him to spell it out to me unless by some weird twist of fate he names his food.

He wipes a paper napkin across his lips. "That's her. Maisy. We dated for a couple of years."

I'm grateful that I ordered soup. I can't imagine anything heavier in my stomach right now. I push the spoon into the bowl and twirl it within the ribbon noodles and vegetables. "Have you heard from her since that night?"

I don't care if he has. I'm trying to be polite and short of asking him whether he's planning on getting back together with her, I don't know the right way to react. I've known him for only a few days. I've shared the most intense intimate experiences of my life with him and he's been nothing but honest and open with me. Why should it matter that he's talking about Maisy?

He places the rest of the sandwich on the plate in front of him. "You're the opposite of her."

That's not even remotely close to being an answer to my question but I'm actually relieved. I don't want to know if she's whimpering somewhere off in the distance because she wants to be back in his arms and bed. I can't imagine a scenario in which she's not torn apart by his rejection. There's a very real, and almost guaranteed, chance that this intense attraction between us will eventually hit a brick wall and we will part ways. I know that and I know even now that it will sting.

"What's she like?" I half expect him to scowl at the question.

"Smart, driven. I'd say she's focused," he begins before he takes a heavy swallow from the glass of beer he ordered with his dinner. "She works on Wall Street in finance."

"Where did you meet?" My mouth thinks that's a good question apparently. It didn't give my mind time to tell it to shut the hell up.

He tugs at the collar of his shirt. "We met at a bar. There's no story there. I saw her, bought her a drink and the rest is history."

"Why did you bring her up?" I can hear the coolness in my own voice.

He finishes the glass of beer in one mouthful. He places it down with a dull thud on the table as his mouth thins into a line. "She wants me back. She came to see me at work yesterday."

A week ago I would have passed him on the street with a twist of my neck for an extra glance because he's so attractive. Now, I'm sitting here listening to him telling me that the woman he's been involved with for the past two years, wants him again. I'm not shocked. Sadness doesn't factor into what I'm feeling. I got to enjoy him for a few days in what has always been an ordinary life. How can I not take that experience and embrace it? He's not mine to have. I know that. I've known it since I took him into my bed.

"You're a class act." I push my hands against the edge of the table readying myself to stand. "Most guys wouldn't have gone to this much trouble to set things straight."

"Don't move, Bridget. Don't walk away from me. I won't let you do it."

"I can't do it, Dane. I won't fuck a guy if he has a girlfriend."

"Have you ever been in love?"

I remind myself that I'm talking to a man I only met mere days ago. I don't know anything about him beyond the fact that he's a fireman and he has a natural talent for fucking a woman senseless. I have no idea how old he is or where he was born. I don't know if he likes going to the movies, or if he even watches television. I know that twirling my tongue around the wide crest of the head of his cock, pulls a growl from deep within him that doesn't normally exist there. I know that he moans as he's tonguing me to orgasm. I know that when he slides his body into mine, it feels like everything in the entire world has stopped for those moments.

"Bridget?" he hesitates for a heartbeat before he continues. "You're twenty-three. You've been in love, haven't you?"

I could lie and say that I have, but I haven't. "No. I've never been in love."

His mouth softens and his eyes catch mine across the table. "I was in love once."

*With Maisy.*

I know that those are the words that will follow. He'll speak about connections and bonds that are forged through good and bad times. He'll talk about investing in her and the growth that they've seen in one another. He'll say things that I'll carry with me until I find a man to love.

"You're in love with Maisy." The words spill from me so quickly they jam into one another in a twisted mess.

His brow furrows as he tries to decipher what I just said. "I loved Maisy."

It's a slight difference that has no place when you've just ended a relationship. Love can shift into something else in the blink of an eye but when you're standing on the precipice of letting it go, sliding back into it is easy. I know from experience. Not my own, of course, but a man I felt things for. They were feelings that held the promise of more until he left me to go back to the woman he cared for before he met me.

I smooth my hands over the fabric of my jeans as I lower my head. "You love Maisy. I get that. You don't owe me anything. I barely know you."

"You know me better than she ever did."

The low hum of his words brings my head up in a flash. I stare at his face. "I don't know anything about you."

"You know that I can't stay away from you," he says confidently. "You know that I want you in a way I've never wanted a woman before."

I don't know that. I want to know that. "You don't know me. We barely know each other."

He pushes aside the utensils and dishes that litter the table between us. I stare down at his hands, knowing he wants me to rest mine in them. I do because I crave his touch right now. I know it will ground me even if I'm not sure that I'll walk out of this diner with him in my life.

"When I met Maisy I saw something in her," he pauses to look at his shaky hands. "I guess I saw stability, and a future. We're the same age and we both wanted the same things."

"How old are you?"

"I'm twenty-nine. I haven't told you that?"

"No." I look away suddenly feeling foolish for having such little knowledge of man I've shared so much of my body with. "I didn't ask before."

"I turned twenty-nine this week." His eyes are dark and haunting. "I looked across the table in that restaurant at Maisy. I realized that I was living my life for her and not myself."

I look past his shoulder to the entrance of the diner. People are filing in and out as they would do on any given day. They're oblivious to the conversation that the two of us are having. "Did you fall out of love with her?"

"At some point I did." His voice is husky. "I was going through the motions but that night I realized that spending another year of my life with her would kill me inside."

I want to be mature and say the things that aren't expected. I want to know if she's beautiful. I'm craving the details about what he said to her at that table but those answers won't change anything. They will only feed my need to know about things that aren't my concern. They are moments and experiences that belong to Dane and Maisy, not to anyone else.

"I've been craving something more for months, Bridget."

"Why did you wait so long to leave her then?" I know the question is direct and maybe even rude given the fact that he's essentially pouring out his heart to me. "You did it on your birthday."

"That's an easy question to answer." His fingertips glide across the palm of my hand. "I saw you across the restaurant and my entire life changed."

# TEN

Men don't say things like that to me. Until now, the most romantic thing that a man has ever said to me was when Elliott, my boss at the pub, told me he thought I was breathtaking. He had been doing shots with a group of friends of his, so that could have accounted for some of his sentimentality that night. It didn't matter at the time. I'd clung to those words and the promise they held until the day we both realized that we made much better friends, than lovers.

"You left Maisy for me?" Shit. That sounded incredibly too egotistical. That's not even remotely close to what he said. It's not in the same ball park. "I mean, you didn't leave your girlfriend just because you saw me across a restaurant."

"You're right," he confirms quickly. "I was going to break up with her regardless but I saw you and realized that there's a lot more out there. You've helped me see that life is full of possibilities."

I've never been the shoulder to cry on for a man fresh out of a relationship. I've been there for female friends but that's a different dynamic. With them, I cradled them in my arms and consoled them by agreeing with their emotional tirades about how the man they loved was a lying asshole. With Dane, I gave my body to him because I needed his just as much.

I could say something about being glad I could help him out but that would sting me more than it would sting him. I'm his bridge to the other side of his pain. Once the emotional dust has settled and he can see beyond the end of his relationship with Maisy, I'll turn into a reminder of that and he'll need to move on. I can sense it.

"I know that you're probably not looking for something serious. I'm not either." His hands drop mine as he says the words. "I'd like to hang out sometimes. I mean, if you're up for that."

*He'd like to fuck if I'm up for that. There's no masking that.*

"Sure," I try to sound as non-invested in this as I can. "Hanging out with you is fun."

*Translation: I like your tongue, Dane. I like it A LOT.*

"Great," he says in such a loud tone that it not only startles me, but the people at the table next to us jump too. "I'll stop by after you're done your shift tonight."

I know a booty call even when it's blocked its number. He's trying to shelter his desire to slide his cock balls deep into my body by hiding it behind the veil of a friendship. "I can't tonight. I'm going to a club with a few of the girls from work."

It's not a lie. One of the girls at work just moved to New York and in an effort to build some new connections, she'd invited the entire pub to a club in Times Square. I agreed to go because other than the date with Larry and the stolen moments in my bedroom with Dane, my social calendar has been empty.

"You'll have a great time," he says with a grin. "You can tell me all about it the next time I see you."

I smile at the promise of a next time before I pick up my spoon and eat the rest of my now tepid soup.

***

"What do you think Maisy is short for?" I stretch my legs out in front of me. "I've been trying to figure it out for two days and I'm stuck."

"Is this for a crossword puzzle?" Zoe follows my lead and pushes her legs out from underneath her. "You know they always have all the answers to the puzzle in the newspaper the next day."

I turn to look at her. She'd invited me over to her apartment for a spa day as she called it. It's been nothing more than the two of us painting each other's fingernails and drinking cocktails. It's my one day off this week and I couldn't think of anyone I'd want to spend it with more than Zoe. I might have considered Dane if I didn't feel the need to catch my breath.

The man is dangerously addictive and now that I have more understanding about what happened between him and his girlfriend, I realize that he needs time. He may not think he does but I doubt, given my limited experience, that a person can walk away from someone they loved for two years without some lingering feelings.

"It's not a crossword puzzle." I take another sip of my drink. "It's someone's name."

"You know someone named Maisy? Is that like Daisy but with an M?"

"It's like Daisy with an M." I peer at her over the rim of the glass. "Do you think it is short for something?"

"Who do you know with a name like that? Is it someone from the pub?"

This is part of the charm that is Zoe Beck. I ask her a very straightforward question and it turns into something that becomes an hour long interrogation. It happened when I asked her what she thought about hair extensions. I've never gotten them and I owe that to Zoe. She talked me out of it after I asked her if I looked better with or without my hair in a ponytail. The woman knows how to drill down to the heart of the matter. It's no wonder she's studying to be a defense attorney.

"She doesn't work at the pub. She works in finance on Wall Street."

She cranes her neck to the side so she can stare at me directly. "Why didn't you say that in the first place?"

I don't have an answer for that. "I was just curious. She's a friend of a friend and I was wondering what she's like."

"She's the ex of the stranger who comes to your apartment at night to fuck you, isn't she?"

As a matter of fact, yes she is. "He doesn't come to my apartment at night to fuck me anymore. I mean, it's not just that. We had dinner together the other night."

"That's a good sign." She doesn't glance up from her smartphone. Her perfectly manicured fingernail is tapping something out on it. "Are you two dating now?"

"No," I admit. "We're going to take it slow. Hang out sometimes."

"You're keeping your options open." She pats my knee. "I like that."

I press my back into the leather office chair I'm sitting in. We'd come into Zoe's home office after having lunch. She wanted to read over a case file that was assigned to her by her professor and I'd agreed to listen to her arguments. I know little about the law but I was definitely impressed with how persuasive she was.

"There's no Maisy working on Wall Street." She drops her phone into her lap. "I searched and came up empty."

I don't have the heart to tell her that I did the same thing last night. I wasn't expecting to find much and I was actually grateful when I found nothing at all.

"It doesn't matter," I say honestly. "He's a guy I have fun with. There's something else I wanted to talk to you about."

"Can it wait?" She tilts her head to the left just as I hear the baby cry. "I need to check on Vane."

I can't compete with that. I wouldn't want to. I'll have to wait to ask Zoe if she can talk to her husband about looking at my drawings.

# ELEVEN

"Did you have fun at the club?"

I smile at him. "I did. I didn't have as much fun as some of my co-workers."

His brows jump in response. "What does that mean?"

It means when we went to the club at Hotel Aeon in Times Square we walked into a room filled with people all looking for one thing. One of the girls I work with wasted no more than ten minutes before she was practically sitting in a random guy's lap sucking his tongue into her mouth.

I had a drink, refused more than a few offers for another and left before two in the morning. It should be my scene considering I'm single, young and adventurous, but I felt completely out of place there. I couldn't wait to get home and into my bed.

"Nothing," I say in an effort to change the subject. "How have you been?"

It's been four days since I had dinner with Dane. He's texted me twice to catch up and although our exchanges have been friendly and fun, I've been left with a deep sense of longing when they've ended. I like him. I like him too much given the fact that we met only a couple of weeks ago.

"I've been good." He takes a sip of the beer he ordered when he came into the pub an hour ago. "You've been avoiding me."

I haven't. Maybe I have been. After our conversation the other night, I'd called home to talk to my mom. I'd told her sparse details about a man I met and she warned me to keep my head in the game of my own life. She's right and now that I've decided to at least talk to Zoe about my drawings I feel the promise of new possibility.

"I haven't been avoiding you, Dane." I look across the table at him. He's still dressed in his work clothes. He rakes his hand through his short brown hair, which causes his bicep to bulge. I stare at it, remembering when he had me wrapped in his arms in my apartment.

"You like fucking me, don't you, Bridget?"

I almost inhale my own breath into my lungs. I look around, certain that some of the women sitting at the table next to us must have heard him. "You know that I do."

"You think I'm using you to get over Maisy." His eyes bore into me and I feel like a caged animal who is about to be pounced on. "I'm not."

"I don't know if you are," I begin before I stop to consider what I'll say next. "I had a lot of fun with you. I want to have that fun again. I just don't want to get caught up in the middle of your break up."

"My relationship with her is done." He skims his hand over the leg of his pants. "She knows it's over. I know it's over. That's the end of it."

There's no reason for me not to believe him. I don't know him well enough to read between the lines of the nuances in his voice. I do know that there's a flash of tenderness behind his eyes when he looks at me after he's come inside of me. I know that there's compassion in his voice when he asks how I am.

"I believe you," I say quietly. "I just know, from my own limited experience, that break ups can be tough."

"Not this one." He raises his ass off the stool he's sitting in to pull it around the table until he's right next to me. "I told you about Maisy because I want to get to know you better. It was the right thing to do."

It's the words a decent guy would say when he's trying to forge a new connection. He's almost too good to be true which sends up countless warning flags for me. I'm not risking a thing if I keep it casual though. We can have fun, we can fuck and if he happens to realize he's still madly in love with his ex, I'll walk away knowing I didn't let myself fall for him.

***

"Lean forward, Bridget." His voice is needy and deep.

"Like this," I say as I rest my head against the wall. "God, yes, please."

He's behind me. We're both in my bedroom. After I brought him home with me, we'd kissed on the chair we fucked in that first night. He'd held me on his lap while he tongued and licked my mouth until I was so wet; I had to pull my panties off.

Then he'd stripped his clothes off as I yanked the box of condoms out of my bedside table, spilling them all onto the floor. He'd crouched to scoop one into his hand, with his hard cock dangling between his legs. My breath had gotten stuck at the sheer beauty of his body.

Once he was sheathed, he'd pushed me face first into the wall. He grabbed hold of my neck when he slid inside of me and now, resting against each other, I know that within moments, he's going to fuck me from behind until I come all over his cock.

"I love fucking you." His teeth skim over the flesh of my shoulder. "Your body is amazing. It's so perfect. You're so tight."

I reach back to try and capture his lips with mine. I'm rewarded with a deep and sensual kiss. His hand pushes down on my groin, angling my body to take more of him.

"My cock fills you up." It's a statement born from the lust we both feel. "I can feel how deep it goes."

"So deep," I try to form the words but I can't be sure they come out as anything that's even remotely audible.

"My body has ached for this." He pushes his hand down farther until his fingers glide over my clit. "I've thought about it constantly."

I push back wanting him to pulse himself into me. I'm close but I know the moment I feel the friction and hear his labored breathing, I'll be lost to the climax.

"Ah, fuck, Bridget." His hands both fall to my hips as he starts his tender assault. "You're too good. It's all too good."

I rest my head against the wall as I moan loudly with each thrust of his heavy, thick cock into my tender core.

***

"Do you want to draw me?" His breath is against my lips.

My eyes dart open to lock on his. He'd carried me to the bed after he'd tied the used condom and tossed it into the wastebasket. After laying me gently on my back, he stretched out, his head resting between my legs, as he tongued me slowly and painfully to an exquisite release.

Now, we're next to one another, each determined to catch our breath. It's nearing morning, which means he'll leave soon.

"I've never drawn anyone I know before." I reach up to cup his cheek in my palm. I can feel the intimacy that's there floating in the air between us. "I don't know if I could do it."

"I'd love if you'd do it." His lips brush over my neck. "I would be so honored."

I press my lips to his. "I'll think about it."

"You'll think about it and then you'll do it." He slides his hand to the back of my head as he tilts my head to the side to deepen the kiss.

# TWELVE

"Have you thought about showing your drawings to Beck?" Vanessa pulls her hair into a ponytail. "If you say you haven't, I'm going to tell you that you should."

I stare at the back of her head. In passing, you might mistake us for sisters. Our hair color is almost the same, so is our height but the similarities end there. Her smile is wider, her eyes set farther apart and they're a deeper shade of blue. She looks European and although I know she was adopted, I don't know all of the details about her birth family. Zoe has told me bits and pieces and I've expressed an open invitation to talk if she needs it. Vanessa and I aren't as close as Zoe and I but I'm working on changing that. I like being around her. She's positive and bright.

"I was going to talk to Zoe about it, but the timing wasn't right."

"There's an open show at a gallery in SoHo for local artists." She adjusts the silver chain around her neck. "One of the other nurses was talking about it. Her daughter is apparently incredibly gifted. She does sculptures. I thought it might be a good place for you to show some stuff too."

It's an idea that catches me so off guard that I have to take a minute to actually digest it fully. "I don't think I'm ready for something like that yet."

"You are." She turns to look at me. "I can tell that you are."

"It's not that easy," I begin before I stop myself.

"It's open to anyone in Manhattan who wants to show their work so you're actually perfect for it." She completely ignores my comment and I'm grateful for it.

I've wandered through some of the city's galleries when I've had time to kill. Part of the draw has been just to bask in the immense talent that is found in the city but another part of it has been based purely in inspiration. The thought that I could one day have my own drawings hanging in a space where people can come see them is overwhelming.

"I want to hear more about it."

"That's my girl." She pats me on the shoulder. "I'll get you the details and you'll submit a few drawings to see if you're accepted."

I nod. "That's simple. I can do that."

"I know you can." She motions towards the door of her apartment. "Let's go meet Zoe. I'm starving."

***

After I'd finished lunch with Zoe and Vanessa, I went to the park. I haven't drawn in days and the need to create had almost consumed me. I'd rushed home to gather my sketchpad and pencils and set out with a renewed purpose to channel everything I'm feeling inside.

I settle onto the corner of a bench as I see an elderly couple do the same several feet away from me. They're ideal in that their expressions complement one another perfectly as they share stories that are too far off in the distance for me to hear but close enough for me to capture with my hand.

I sketch them both until they stand. I hurry to finish the outline of the drawing wanting to reflect everything I see between them before they wander off into the distance. I touch up the delicate features of their faces as I remember them in my mind's eye for the next hour.

I close my pad realizing that now is the time. I've worked for years to create portraits as a way to channel my view of the world. If I don't put myself out there now, when I have the perfect opportunity to do it, I'll regret it.

I tap out a quick text message to Vanessa reminding her to send me the information about the showing in SoHo. Then I pull up Dane's contact information and type out a text to him telling him that I want to see him.

I'm about to put everything I am out into the world and the feeling of fear mixed with exhilaration makes me realize it's something I've been craving for as long as I can remember.

# THIRTEEN

"You can't move so much, Dane." I hold tight to the edge of my sketchpad. "I need you to stay still."

He stares up into my face. I can't tell what he's thinking. I'd instructed him to lie flat on his back on my bed after we'd made love. His hair is a twisted mess from my fingers pulling on it when he sucked and licked me to my release. His face and chest are flushed from when he crawled up my body and fucked me hard as he held tight to my hips. He's as handsome in this moment as any man I've ever laid eyes on. He's beautiful; he's tender and there's unspoken vulnerability within his expression right now that makes me want to capture it forever.

"How am I supposed to stay still when you're sitting on top of me naked?"

I bow my head down as a smile courses over my lips. I'm straddling his large frame. My wetness is resting against the top of his groin. I'm peering down at him as I try to draw the man who has brought me to the edge of ecstasy time and time again tonight.

"Please don't move," I whisper into the stillness of my apartment. "I love the way you look right now."

He rests his left arm over his head, which only makes him look that much stronger and powerful. "I love the way you look all the time."

"You say those things to throw me off." I gaze down at the sketchpad as I pull the tip of the pencil across it, trying to capture the curve of his jawline.

He cocks a dark brow as his right hand slides to my thigh. "I say those things because I mean them. I don't know a woman who is more beautiful than you are."

They're words that can easily pull me away from what I'm doing. I'm tempted to drop the sketchpad so I can slide down his body and take him in my mouth. I've craved the strong taste of his release since that night weeks ago. I've wanted it again and as soon as I'm done I'm going to take it was my reward.

"Can I have the portrait when you're done?" His hand inches even higher up my thigh.

I feel a sense of loss at the idea of giving it to him. I've never given any of my portraits to anyone which I know isn't the basis for a career based on selling my art. I have to learn to let them go and it seems apropos that his should be the first I gift. I want to show it in SoHo though, if I'm accepted. "I might get to show some of my work at a small gallery. I thought maybe I could show this one."

His face softens at the suggestion and his hands stalls on its path up my thigh towards my core. "You want to show it? You're telling me that you're going to show some of your work in a gallery?"

Bending forward I press my lips to his. "I'm going to submit a few pieces for consideration. If they choose me, I'll get a chance to display my work."

"Bridget, that's amazing." His lips curve into a smile. "I'd be so honored if you used my portrait for that."

"You can have it after that." I straighten back up. "I want you to have it."

"I'll treasure it forever." His chest heaves with the words. "I'll cherish it until the day I die."

***

"My shifts are changing next month." He kisses me softly on the forehead before he pulls the t-shirt he was wearing earlier back over his head. "I'll be working at night for a few weeks."

I don't immediately respond. It's not that I'm not interested in his job. I've never personally known a fireman before and although we don't talk about it much, I find it fascinating and alluring. He's about as perfect as a man can get and the knowledge that he's devoted his life to helping others makes him even that much more irresistible to me.

"I'll have to go home to crash for a few hours every day but we'll still have time to hang out before you go to work at the pub."

In that one sentence, he's succinctly answered every question I may have had. I like spending time with him and the more we do it, the more I want it. Neither of us has said anything about dating one another exclusively but it's hard to imagine sharing my body with another man when I know the promise of Dane's is waiting for me whenever I want it.

"I'll need to finish the portrait." I gesture to where I dropped my sketchbook on the bed. "I'd like to try in daylight. Do you think we could hang out in Central Park when you have a day off?"

"I'll hang out wherever you want me to." He pulls a sweatshirt over his head to cover the t-shirt. "I could stare at you for hours, Bridget."

"That will make it easy for me to draw you then."

He laughs before he leans down and slides his lips over mine.

# FOURTEEN

"It's a breathtaking space." I circle on my heel to soak in the natural light that is pouring in through the floor-to-ceiling windows. "It's perfect, isn't it?"

As I look around I entertain fleeting thoughts of my portraits framed and hung on these walls. It's a life dream coming to fruition and even though she called me earlier to tell me that I'd made the short list of potential artists who will be invited to show their work, I'm feeling confident that I will be chosen and that within weeks I'll be standing in this spot looking at my portraits on the walls.

"I just need you to sign one of these release forms, Bridget." She balances a pen between her index finger and her thumb. "Read it over carefully and then sign at the bottom."

I should ask Vanessa's fiancé, Garrett, to look over the document but as I scan it, I realize there's little that I don't completely understand. I don't need a lawyer for this. It's a standard form granting the gallery rights to showcase my work in any advertisements they may produce in relation to the showing. Judging by what's written within the document, they're planning on doing a media blitz that includes both print and online. I catch my breath as I sign, thinking about the possibility that an image of one of my drawings may appear on the gallery's website.

"Your work is brilliant." She takes the pen from me after I sign my name. "I was quite taken with it."

I know that she can't tell me if I've been chosen. Although her name is on the front of the gallery's awning, the panel of judges is comprised of critics, artists and the people who keep this gallery afloat. They are the benefactors who see art, in all its forms, as an integral part of life.

"I'm honored that I was chosen as a finalist," I say with all sincerity. I was actually initially shocked when I'd received the call that my work had made it through the review process. The gallery is going to be showcasing four different artists. There are ten finalists so I know my chances are good.

"You're available for the unveiling ceremony?"

"Yes, Mrs. Boudreau. I am."

"We'll be in touch then." I watch her head as it turns towards the door where a blonde haired young man is standing in wait. "That's another candidate. I'll need to get to him."

I nod as I take one last look at the space that may change my life forever.

***

"I'm not sure how to tell you this." His eyes don't meet mine as he says the words.

My heart stalls for a full beat and the pencil in my hand stops moving on the paper. I don't want the next thing that comes out of his mouth to be about Maisy. He hasn't brought her up since that night weeks ago. I haven't either. If he mentions her now it's going to derail me completely. "What is it?"

He rakes his hand through his hair, pushing it into a mess that makes him look boyish in a way that only compliments his face. "I'm crazy about you."

I feel a smile tug at the corner of my lips as I allow my lungs to fill with air again. "You're crazy about me?"

His gaze flicks over my face. "I'm really crazy about you, Bridget."

"You weren't sure how to tell me that?" I look back down at the sketch and bring the pencil to his hairline. "Why weren't you sure about that?"

"I don't know how you feel about me." He nods towards the sketchpad. "I know you're addicted to my good looks and charm but I'm more than a pretty face."

I pull the pad up to cover the wide grin on my mouth. "I know that you are."

"I met you at exactly the right time in my life." He scratches the side of his nose as he turns to look across the park. "I'm a lucky guy."

"I'm a lucky girl," I say under my breath.

"I heard that." A ghost of a grin pulls at the edge of his full lips. "When we get back to your apartment, I'll show you exactly how lucky you are."

# FIFTEEN

"Your body was made for me. It feels so good to fuck you."

I can't argue that point. Right now I can't even agree with that point. He's already brought me to an orgasm with just the touch of his hands. I'm underneath him, flat on my back while he hovers above me. My eyes fall to the tattoo on his chest and I study the words, trying to capture them within my mind so I can search for them later.

"My mother wrote poetry." He glances down my body. "She writes poetry."

It's a glimpse into the family he never speaks of. I don't fault him for that. I don't talk about my parents either. We're not at a point where people, beyond the two of us, matter enough to pull them into every day conversations. I like dwelling on him when I'm with him. I love watching the way his lips move when he talks about the calls he went out on that day. I grip tightly to his body when he's giving me pleasure and I feel bereft when he kisses me goodnight and walks out the door.

"Is that her poetry?" I glide my fingers across his chest and over the words. "Did she write that for you?"

"In a way," he whispers. "It's her handwriting."

"She wrote on your chest." I furrow my brow as I follow the delicate lines of the tattoo.

"No." He shakes his head slightly causing the motion to transfer into his shoulders and torso. "She wrote it on a paper for me. The tattoo artist I saw... he... he transferred it to me."

It's a lasting tribute to a woman who obviously means the world to him. "I like that. I like knowing that."

"I love my mother." He smiles as he stares into my eyes. "One day I hope you can meet her."

It's something that I hope for too. It may be far off in the distance but I can see it on the horizon now. "I'd love to meet her."

"You'll have to meet Garrett's mother too." He winks. "My mom and his mom are sisters. They're thick as thieves. One never goes anywhere without the other."

I scan his face, wanting to tell him that I'm feeling things for him that I can't express yet, but they're there waiting for the right moment. "Your family sounds amazing, Dane."

"Not as amazing as you." He shifts his legs so his swollen cock brushes against my groin. "You came out of nowhere and changed everything."

I close my eyes as he lowers his soft lips to mine and I drink in not only the taste of him, but also the meaning of his words.

***

"You don't have any hot water." He rubs a white towel over his damp hair as I turn over in bed to look at him. It's morning and the fact that he's showered means he stayed the night with me again. "I'm colder now than when I went in to have a shower."

I wince at the thought of him taking a shower in the frigid water that typically comes out of the taps at this time of day. "Most of the people who live in the building shower around this time every morning so I always wait a couple of hours."

"Thanks for the heads-up," he says teasingly. "I'm clean. That's all that matters."

It's not all that matters. It's a perfect segue into a topic I've been meaning to ask him about since he started staying over at my place. "I can come over to your place sometimes. I'd like to see where you live."

The muscles in his bare back tighten at the suggestion. His hands freeze in place before he slides the towel from his hair and dries his body. "That's not going to work right now, Bridget."

I teeter on the edge of his response for more than a minute. He doesn't offer anything more so I dive right in because of that promise I'd made myself after he told me about Maisy. I won't get pulled into the middle of anything he has going on with her. She's not a factor in my life and if the magnetic pull that initially drew him to her is still there, he needs to tell me now. "Why not?"

Maybe he's never been questioned point blank before or perhaps he's always fallen back on his skills as a lover to draw a woman's attention away from the issue at hand because there's hesitation in his stance. He turns slowly to face me. "I'd love to fuck you once more before I leave."

*No. Don't. Please don't say that.*

"I'm all fucked out right now." I pull on the blanket that he'd kicked to the foot of the bed when he mounted me last night. "Answer the question please."

He watches as I cover my breasts with the blanket, tucking it under my ass. "Please don't over react."

Again, he's drawing assumptions based on his past experience. If I over react, he'll retreat behind a shield of lies. He'll tell me what he thinks will quiet my suspicions enough that he can find the nearest exit. I'll never know the truth and when he walks out he'll take the promise of what might have been with him. "I won't."

He scrubs his hand over the back of his neck before he lowers himself to the edge of the bed. "It's Maisy. She still lives at my place."

# SIXTEEN

It's brutally true what they say about perfection being non-existent. It's not that I thought Dane was perfect. He's not. I'm not. It's a fantasy that people think exists when they can't bear the thought of accepting someone for who they are.

"You live with her?" I look him straight in the eye while I struggle to control my tone. "You live with your ex-girlfriend?"

He reaches towards me. My first instinct is to recoil but I sit in place. "I don't live with Maisy."

"You just said that she lives at your place," I point out as I slide my ass slightly to the left. I need distance so I can find clarity. "Does she live at your place or not?"

"I bought a house in Queens five years ago." He looks up at the ceiling as he swallows hard. "I asked her to move in with me a few months after we started dating."

The words don't sting. I wasn't in the picture then. I've known him less than a month so I can't whimper over the fact that almost two years ago he asked a woman that he loved to share his home and his bed with him.

"I've asked her to leave but she hasn't." He taps his feet against the floor. "Most of my stuff is still there. I go back once a week when she's at work if I need anything."

"Why won't she leave?"

"Her father's a lawyer." He looks at the window and into the soft morning light streaming through it. "She wants part of it."

I don't want to get into the details of his finances. That's definitely not my business and it would create an awkward imbalance in our relationship. He's never asked me about my own financial situation. It may be bleak and uninspiring, but it's private. We're nowhere near close enough to delve into the inner workings of each other's long term financial goals.

"Do you have someone to help you with that?" I ask because it's polite, not because I can offer any suggestions in the form of lawyers, other than his cousin.

"We're working it out."

I don't ask for clarification. I don't want it. I just want to understand one thing. "Is there a chance that you and Maisy are going to work things out? Do you think you'll move back in with her at some point?"

There's not a beat of hesitation in his voice as he turns directly towards me. "Never. I will never spend another day of my life with her."

***

"If you don't live with her, where do you live?" I look at where he's standing. He's fully dressed now, his hands tucked into the front pockets of his jeans.

"I don't live anywhere." He shrugs his shoulders as his gaze falls to the floor. "I stay with friends. Sometimes I crash at work. I have a duffel bag of clothes. Everything else is at the house."

I have an empty bedroom and an almost drained bank account because I can barely keep up with the rent. For a brief moment the notion of asking him to move in, enters my mind but it's gone before I can give it any credence.

"Are you going to look for a place to live?"

"I have a place to live, Bridget." His fingers brush mine as he reaches towards the bed to scoop his smartphone into his hand. "I need her to leave so I can move back in."

"I understand," I say without looking at him.

"Look, I need to get to work." He leans down to graze his lips over my forehead. "I'll call you this afternoon."

I know he will. He always does what he says but suddenly that doesn't feel like it's enough.

# SEVENTEEN

"Beck had all kinds of crazy ex-girlfriends," Zoe stops to adjust her skirt. "Actually, there was only one who I'd classify as bat shit crazy. That was Liz."

I don't know who she's talking about and frankly I don't care. I didn't ask Zoe to walk down to the café at the corner with me so I could hear about her husband's dating past. If I wanted to know that, I'd type his name into Google. I did it once and the sheer volume of the image results of him with different women he was with before he met Zoe, made me want to disinfect my laptop.

"I can check into his rights regarding the house," she offers as she pulls open the door to the café. It's just past ten in the morning so the crowd has thinned considerably. Trying to grab a coffee in a spot like this early in the day is like maneuvering your way around a minefield. It's quieted enough now that there's an empty table in the corner.

"Go grab that table and I'll order for us." I wave my finger towards the corner. "What do you want?"

"I should have herbal tea." Her eyes scan the menu. "I'll have something with lots of espresso and some whipped cream on top."

I shake my head as I giggle aloud. "Go sit. I'll get our drinks and I'll be right there."

***

"You draw?" Her eyes dart across my face before they settle on my hands.

I was surprised that I got the words out. I'd listened to her tell me about the woman who lives in the apartment below her. She replayed each and every conversation the two of them have ever shared in the elevator. Once she quieted enough that I knew she was done, I threw it out there. I told her that I had spent the majority of my life drawing pencil portraits and that I'm a finalist for a gallery showing.

"I do." I pull my smartphone into my palm. "I took some pictures of some of the drawings before I left my apartment. I wanted to show you."

She reaches greedily for the phone as her fingers dance across the screen. "Bridget, you drew these?"

I nod even though I know she can't see the movement of my head because her eyes are so focused on the drawings. "I've drawn them forever. I have hundreds of them."

"Why have you never told me?"

The disappointment that I feared might be in her voice is there. Zoe's not creative in the same way that I am or that her husband is. She's brilliant at reading people and providing a level headed voice when all reason flies out the window.

"I was scared I think," I say honestly. "I was worried that if I showed them to you that you'd show them to Beck and he'd tell me in that sweet way that he has that it's a good hobby for me, but the potential for more doesn't exist."

"You may be more talented than my husband." A smile tugs at the corner of her mouth. "Seriously, Bridget. Why the hell have you been hiding these away?"

Her words cut to my core. I know that she's teasing but I know that it's all based in shock. "Dane helped me to see that it was time to share them."

"Dane is my hero." She hands me back my phone. "You need to bring some of these over to show Beck. Promise me you'll do that."

"I promise." I slide my phone back into my bag. "You have to promise me something too."

"Anything." She finishes the last sip of her coffee. "What is it?"

"Don't tell him about the gallery contest. He knows everyone in the art world. I want to do this all by myself."

"I won't say a word. I don't need to. You're going to get a spot in that show and a year from now, you'll have a gallery showing devoted to just your work."

# EIGHTEEN

"I want you to do something for me, Bridget." He grips tightly to the bottle of beer in his hands. "I should say that I want to ask you to do something."

He had sent me a text message earlier asking if it would be okay for him to come see me at work. I couldn't say no and it wasn't because I had an insatiable need to see him. We haven't defined our relationship, or friendship, or whatever this is.

We've just been two people who stumbled into each other's lives who have fun with one another. He makes me smile, he likes me exactly as I am and he answers every question I've ever asked him honestly. He's never promised me anything but a good time and he's delivered on that in spades. Turning him down when he reached out to me this afternoon wasn't even an option. I want to hear him out. I owe myself that much.

"What is it?" I glance back to where Elliott's flirting with another server by the bar. He's never gotten on my case when I've taken breaks in the middle of my shift to visit with friends who have dropped in to the pub. He understands and seeing him with his hand on the hip of the brunette who started last week, I know I have nothing to worry about. I can take all time I need with Dane, especially since it's almost closing time.

He sips from the bottle before settling it down carefully. "Before I ask, I want to explain something,"

It's never that easy when a man tells you that he wants you to do something for him. Judging by the anxiety that is forcing his knee to tremble, I'd say that this has nothing to do with sex. "Explain then."

I know I sound harsh and impatient but I'm still absorbing the news that Maisy lives in his house. I've never lived with a man so when my relationships have ended, it's been clean and complete. I can't imagine the emotions that a person has to juggle when they not only walk away from a person they cared for, but they have to divide the fundamental parts of their everyday lives too.

"I think about you pretty much all the time."

I could repeat that right back to him and I'd mean every single word of it. Even now, as I wait for word about the finalists for the gallery show, my thoughts always jump back to his smile, the way he touches my face and the feeling of his lips as they race across my skin.

He hesitates as if he's waiting for me to say something in kind back to him. I can't yet. How can I open myself up to that when there are so many loose ends still at play from his last relationship? I check the calendar that hangs in my bedroom every morning. I know the date. It hasn't been that long since my non-date with Larry which means Dane broke up with his girlfriend just a few weeks ago.

"I don't know that much about how to handle my emotions." He drops his gaze to the table. "I do know what I'm feeling."

I know what I'm feeling too. I know that this may be something that will never cross my path again. I know that people talk about falling in love at first sight or first touch. I'm not subscribing to those theories but I do feel things I've never felt before when I'm near him. I like him, more than I've ever liked anyone in my life. I feel a sense of comfort when I'm in his arms. Once he walks out of my apartment, my body aches for his.

"What do you feel?"

"That I'd sit outside your apartment all day just to get a glimpse of your face," he says quietly. "I feel like if I ever kiss another woman, I'll compare her to you."

I look over his shoulder to the wall behind him because I know that my face will betray the joy I feel in hearing those words.

"I know that when I hear you come, that I'd move heaven and earth to hear it again."

My gaze flicks over his face and I realize he's staring right at me. I pause to lock my eyes with his. "You know I'm unsure. It hasn't been that long since…"

"It hasn't been that long since I ended things with Maisy," he interrupts to finish my thought for me. "That feels like a lifetime ago, Bridget. I don't honestly know what I felt inside before I met you."

I feel as though my chest is going to cave in. It's too fast and too soon. I smooth my hand over my hair hoping that the gesture will give me a reprieve from everything I'm feeling. "You said you wanted to ask me to do something. What is it?"

I can't gauge whether he's taking a moment to consider exactly what he wants to say to me or if he's trying to regain himself after a momentary loss of composure. "I want you to trust me, Bridget. I want a chance to show you that I'm a good and honest man."

It's a request that he doesn't need to make. "I know that you're a good man. I could feel it when you saved my arm from being stolen away by Larry."

His eyes brighten as his hands settle on the table top near me. "You're nothing like anyone I've ever met. You're everything that I never knew I wanted. I just want a chance to see where this is going."

It's romantic and in my world where romance has been fleeting and admittedly, rare, I want to savor the moment and bask it in. My good sense is pulling at me though. "I want to see where it's going too but I need it to be slow."

There's no break in his expression at all. "Then we'll take things slow."

"I should get back to work." I motion towards the empty tables. "I have to wipe these down before I head home."

"I can wait and take you."

I want that. I want to crawl into bed and wrap my naked body around his but I also want to catch my breath. "I think I should be alone tonight."

"I can still ride the subway with you." He picks up the bottle of beer and finishes the last sip. "I won't come inside. I'll just kiss you goodnight at your door."

***

I was the one who almost broke my own request. He'd held my hand on the subway platform before we boarded the train and he wrapped his strong arm around me as I rested my weary head against his chest.

Once he got to the door of my apartment, he'd taken my face in his hands and kissed me softly and sweetly. His tongue dipped between my lips for a minute and I was tempted right then to pull him inside. I want him but not tonight. Tonight I'm going to finish some of the drawings I've begun in the park. My chance to showcase my work is right there within my grasp. Regardless of what happens between Dane and me, I know that I have a future in the art world. I saw proof of that on Zoe's face.

I pull off my clothes and open my sketchbook. I flip the pages until I'm staring into the face of the man who I just kissed goodbye at my door.

I bring my pencil to the paper and focus on his dark eyes as I bring them to life. I plow through the sketch over the course of the next several hours until I finally fall asleep with the sketchpad next to me and the pencil still clutched tightly in my hand.

# NINETEEN

I'm jarred awake by the ever present sound of sirens. It comes with living in Manhattan. When I first moved here, I'd turn to stare each time a police car, ambulance or fire truck sped past me. That habit was short lived once I realized that I as soon as one siren is out of ear's range, another is almost always approaching.

I admit that I do a double take now if a fire truck races past me. I try to spot the Engine Company's number on the side of the truck. I started that the day I sat in front of the fire station Dane works at.

I pull myself out of the bed and wrap my short robe around me. It's too early to shower so I set out on a path to make coffee so I can push the chill I'm feeling out of my body. I'm just taking my first sip when my phone rings.

My heart stalls when I see the name written across the screen. I pull in a heavy breath, clear the sleep from my throat and answer. "Good morning, Mrs. Boudreau."

There's a slight pause before she responds," Bridget, that's you?"

"It's me." Of course it's me. Even though I feel like my life is suspended in some strange vortex of time right now, it's me.

"There's been a decision made."

This is the last second I have to hold onto the hope that I'm going to get to show my drawings in that gallery. I want to believe I'll have the confidence to pursue my art in a more public way now that I know that Vanessa, Zoe and Dane think I'm talented. If the gallery turns me down, I can't let myself falter. I have to believe that there's still a future for me sharing my work with people who'll appreciate the subtle emotion within it.

"It's unanimous," she begins before she stops to rustle some papers near the phone's receiver. You'd think she'd have the answer on the tip of her tongue before she dialed my number. "Congratulations, Bridget. You're in."

I somehow manage to thank her before I disconnect the call, drop my phone on the table and scream at the top of my lungs.

***

"I knew that they'd choose you," he says the words so softly that I have to shift my head slightly just to hear them. "I knew it."

I turn to look at his face. It's the same face that I've been sketching for the past few weeks. I've tried desperately to capture exactly what I see now but that's impossible.

"I'm going to show your portrait there." I pull on his arms to wrap them around my waist. "You're going to be there the night it opens, right?"

"You'll tell me when and I'll make sure I have it off." He glides his leg over my hip. I can feel his arousal pressing into me.

I reach back to kiss him softly before I run my tongue over his bottom lip. "You are the first person I've told. I haven't said a word to any of my friends."

It's a tender confession that means more to me than he may realize.

"I knew by the sound of your voice on the phone that the news was good. I'm so excited people will finally see your talent."

He speaks as if he's been a constant in my life for years. His belief in my ability to draw began the night he saw my portraits for the first time. "I'm excited too."

"You can tell that I'm extra excited." He presses his lips into my neck as he grinds his cock against my ass. "I need to fuck you, Bridget."

I twist around so I'm facing him. I take his head between my hands and I kiss him with all the passion I've felt for him since that moment he locked eyes with me at the restaurant. I pull back to look at him.

"You gave me the courage to show my work to other people." I slide my fingertips down his cheek. "I need to thank you for that."

"You are." His hands fall to my ass. "I'm about to get all the thanks I need."

# TWENTY

"I'm sorry, Bridget." His hands reach towards me but I take a heavy step back.

We're standing on the street outside of my apartment. It's been a week since I found out that my work has been chosen for the gallery show. I've spent parts of each day with Dane after he's gone to a friend's house to sleep. The rest of my time has been filled with going through my portfolio with Brighton to choose the right portraits. He's also helped me frame them.

Zoe went shopping with me to pick out a new dress and I cleaned my apartment from top to bottom knowing that my parents are set to arrive tomorrow right before the unveiling. Everything has fallen into place. Or it was until Dane dropped a bombshell on me just now.

"How can you do that?" I ask knowing that I sound like a spoiled child. "You can't move it to another time?"

He shakes his head as his eyes dart to the ground. "It's the only time Maisy will meet with me. If I blow this off, I may never get my house back."

If I hadn't understood the meaning of being between a rock and a hard place I do now. He had told me last week that he'd switched his night shift with someone at work so that he could be at the gallery standing next to me. I wanted him there not just to offer support on the most important night of my life. I also wanted him to see himself through my eyes.

Tomorrow will be the first time he'll see the portrait I drew of him and I want to be next to him when that happens. It's by far the most personal portrait I've ever completed.

"I think I can still make it to the gallery before they do the actual unveiling."

My eyes dart up to rest on his face. "What time are you meeting her?"

"At five." He takes a step back to allow a woman with a stroller to pass between us. "We're meeting at a lawyer's office in mid-town so once I'm done there I can come straight to the gallery."

I don't know how long it takes for a couple to squabble over a piece of property. Two hours seems like plenty of time but maybe that's just wishful thinking on my part.

"I really want you there." I step towards him. "I know we haven't known each other that long but it would mean a lot to me if you could try and be there by seven."

"I belong there." He leans into me when his arms circle my shoulders. "There's no place I want to be more than with you tomorrow but this is my house. I saved most of my life for it. I can't let her take it away."

"I understand." I rest my head against his chest as the sounds of the city waft through the air around us.

"She's willing to talk. I need to listen."

He falls silent as he clings to me on the crowded sidewalk in the middle of the afternoon.

***

"You're sure you don't mind taking care of my parents?" I study Zoe's face for any wayward signs of regret. "You offered but I wasn't sure if you were being sincere."

"I love hanging out with them." She pushes a piece of my hair behind my ear. "You have to take care of last minute preparations. It doesn't make sense for you to be at the gallery and then come all the way back uptown to get them."

It's pure logic in her mind but that's not quite how I see it. When I'd called my parents to tell them that I'd secured a place in a gallery showing their first question, in unison, while on speakerphone was what was I getting paid to do it?

Nothing about the conversation surprised me beyond my muted replies to them. I was honest when I told them that I wasn't being paid and it was more about exposure and potential than anything else. My mother's sigh and my father's clipped, "I see," were enough to make me instantly regret inviting them.

When I'd told Zoe about the conversation she offered me a way out. She said that she and her husband would send a car to my place to pick up my parents. Once they arrived at Zoe's apartment she promised that she'd keep them occupied with Vane until it was time to leave for the gallery. I'm here to thank her now and to get one last hug of reassurance from her.

"You're going to stun everyone tonight, Bridge."

"I still can't believe this is happening," I say softly as much to her as to myself. "Two months ago I didn't think my drawings would ever see the light of day."

"I'm so proud of you." She lifts her head towards me. "You're taking control of your talent. Your entire life is going to change tonight."

I sense that too. It may be the anticipation that's in the air or it could just be that I feel numb out of fear and apprehension. Either way I know that by the time this night is over, people with know my name and my work.

# TWENTY-ONE

"Are you as bummed as I am?" The blonde haired man I saw at the entrance to this gallery a few weeks away is standing next to me.

I dart my head in his direction and I'm greeted with a smile filled with crooked teeth. It suits him in a sense and I can't help but smile back at him. "I'm bummed too."

I am bummed. There had been a traffic issue two blocks up from where the gallery is. Several city blocks have been cordoned off and since the traffic only runs one way on this street, anyone who wants to get here has to follow a twisted maze on foot. It's just past seven now and the only people who are in the gallery are the other three artists, a reviewer from one of the leading art journals, a caterer, his staff and my friend Vanessa and her fiancé Garrett.

Garrett had asked about Dane the moment he walked into the space and I'd offered the only explanation I can think of. He's trying to get here along with the Becks, and my parents.

Another sudden rush of sirens sends everyone to the windows. We watch as a trio of fire engines race up the street. The flashing lights of a police car following close behind peaks the interest of a few people enough that they venture out into the chilly air to try and grab a closer look.

I take a moment to move across the gallery to a small cabinet where Mrs. Boudreau told me I could lock my purse before she left to go home to change. I doubt that she'll make it back here given what's happening. I decide that it may be best to call her to see if she wants to reschedule or if we should go ahead and talk about our pieces with the one journalist who is here.

"I wonder if Dane got called in to work that emergency." I hear Garrett's voice over my shoulder as I pull my phone free from my purse after unlocking the cabinet.

I glance down. There are three missed calls and four new messages all from Dane.

**I got called in to work. I'm sorry. I'm crazy about you.**

My heart sinks. It's not just that I'm disappointed that he won't be here to share in the most important moment of my life, so far. I'm semi devastated that I won't get to see the expression on his face when he walks through the gallery doors and sees the portrait I did of him.

I don't type anything back because judging by the continual rush of sirens that permeates the air, Dane and every other person responding to that emergency, is in for a long night.

"He's there," I say to Vanessa, even though the words are meant for her and Garrett.

"I'm walking down to take a look." Garrett turns towards both Vanessa and me. "Do either of you want to come?"

I have nothing to lose at this point. One of the other artists is huddled in a corner with the journalist. She's taking advantage of the situation by pointing out every unique nuance that is hidden within her paintings. I'll be able to have my moment to shine tonight too but for now, it looks like I have some time to kill.

"I'll walk down there with you." I wave my hand towards the door.

I grab my coat, wrap it around the beautiful short black dress I'm wearing and lead the way out of the gallery and onto the sidewalk.

***

If I had to describe the scene we came upon a block and a half from the gallery, I would call it muted chaos. There were no flames; no cars had crashed violently into one another. There were several fire engines, ambulances and a sprinkling of police cars that had all seemingly screeched to their halts right in front of a darkened restaurant.

Others had gathered on the sidewalk opposite the building in question to get a better look. I'm not tall, and even in the three inch heels I'm wearing it's hard to see beyond the crowd. I do spot the Engine Company that Dane works for. I see the fire truck with the number thirty-four across the side.

I admit, even in the middle of this scene with all the flashing lights, people running about and the ever approaching sirens in the distance, that I've wondered what Dane looks like in his gear, when he's just about to save a life or put out a fire.

I glance back to where Vanessa and Garrett are standing behind me. I motion towards the street and Garrett instantly understands what I want. I want a front row seat, or in this case, standing position, for the action.

He takes the lead and pushes his way through the gathered crowd until the three of us are standing on the edge of the curb. I can see policemen talking to one another. I see a man in a fireman's helmet barking orders at others. I strain to pick out any words that I can from the various conversations that are taking place.

It's obvious something is happening in the closed restaurant across the street but the space is dark and quiet. It's a direct contrast to what's happening right in front of me.

I scan the names on the backs of the firemen's jackets as they dart past me. I can't quite catch some but when I do, my heart stops, hoping that it's Dane.

We've shared how fond we are of each other, but right now, watching the scene that is unfolding in front of me, I realize how much fear I feel. I've read the stories in the news about firemen who go into a building and don't come out alive. I know that sometimes, even in the most prepared scenarios, that the unexpected can happen and lives are lost.

I turn my head slightly to the left and that's when I spot them. It's two firemen, standing next to one another, their eyes on the building, and their backs turned towards us. I see his name, spelled in bold black letters across the back of his heavy navy blue jacket.

BECKETT.

He's tall, his shoulders are broad and when his left hand darts up to tap the brim of the helmet of another man who approaches them, I see the telling gesture of that gentleman who rescued me from the restaurant a few weeks ago.

Garrett pats me on the shoulder and then points to where Dane is standing. I turn back towards him. "It's him. I see him."

"I'll try and call him over for a minute," he says the words loudly.

I stand in silence staring at Dane's back as I hear Garrett calling his name, not once, but twice.

Dane's head turns to the left before he looks back towards the building. It's as if he heard something but then shook it off.

Garrett yells louder this time and his reward is a definite shift in Dane's stance. He starts to turn and when he does I start frantically waving my hand in his direction. It's misplaced and silly given that we're standing at the scene of an actual emergency.

Dane pushes his helmet back slightly so he can get a clearer view of the gathered crowd. His eyes scan the faces until they come to rest on mine.

"He sees us," Garrett's voice carries over the crowd. "Wave to him, Bridget so he knows it's you."

I do and as he starts to walk towards me, I can't contain my need to touch him. I know he's working, I know it's the complete wrong and inappropriate thing to do but seeing all the emergency personnel that have gathered has hit a chord within me.

Why haven't I realized that he puts himself at risk all the time? I was so focused on a relationship that he willingly ended that I haven't let myself truly get lost in what I'm feeling for him. It might not be love yet, but it's something more than I've ever felt with a man.

He starts to walk towards me in all his gear with a brilliant smile on his face. His arms swing at his sides, his legs take large steps towards me and he looks imposing, heroic and different than he does when he's in my bed at night when the city has quieted.

The space between us feels enormous so in one quick movement I crouch to scoot beneath the yellow tape that is bordering the sidewalk. It's there to keep the crowds at bay but I need to touch him, even if it's just for a minute. I instinctively glance to my right to see if any traffic is coming.

I take a step off the sidewalk and just as I do I look up and see him running.

Dane is coming at me full force, his hands waving in the air. His face has twisted into something I've never seen before. It may be panic or fear.

I take quicker steps wanting to lessen the space between us and that's when I hear him call out to me.

"Bridget. No, stop. Don't."

I freeze. I've never heard his voice at this pitch before and just as I reach out my arms to him, I hear something else. It's a horn.

It's unrelenting, it's piercing and when my head finally turns to the left I feel the impact before my eyes can fully focus on the police car racing towards me.

The pain that shoots through my hip as I'm thrown onto the hood is only quieted when my head smashes into the windshield of the car as it comes to a screeching halt.

I hear screaming in the distance.

I hear my name.

I hear Dane's voice…

And then I hear nothing at all.

# EMBER

## PART TWO

NEW YORK TIMES &
USA TODAY BESTSELLING AUTHOR
DEBORAH BLADON

# ONE

"Bridget? I don't think she can hear me. She's not responding to me at all."

That's true. I can't deny it. I'm not responding to her voice at all. It has nothing to do with the fact that I was hit by a police car four weeks ago. It has everything to do with the fact that my mother has taken on a personal mission to point out how every decision I've made the past few months has contributed to the fact that I ended up on that street right in the path of that car.

I don't remember much about that night. I remember panicked cries, although I'm still not sure if they were coming from my body or not. The pain drowned everything out. It enveloped me and I couldn't pinpoint exactly where it began or where it ended. It was just there, unrelenting and vast.

Dane had been there, yelling at people to back away so no one would move me. I landed on the hood of the car, my scalp covered in a matted mess of my own hair, shattered glass and blood.

I lost consciousness for only a few minutes, which was both a blessing and a curse. My voice had gotten lost somewhere in my throat so the only way I was able to communicate with the first responders was by a nod of my head. They took that as a positive sign and when I was able to freely move my legs and arms there was a sense of relief that washed over Dane's face and the faces of the paramedics.

The police officer who was behind the wheel of the car that hit me was racing towards the scene of the emergency that had brought Dane and dozens of other firefighters to that block in SoHo. He had slowed the car as soon as he saw me dart onto the road but the impact was unavoidable. I had been lucky. That's what the doctors in the ER had told me over and over again.

I'd spent a week in the hospital recovering from three broken ribs, a fractured wrist, a concussion, and numerous small cuts on my scalp and face. In the days following the accident my thoughts were so muddled that I struggled to remember the first moments after my parents arrived at the hospital and the look on Zoe's face when she saw me on the stretcher. The dress she had bought for me was torn and stained. My bloody hand had reached for hers and without hesitation she had cradled it between her palms before pulling it to her chest.

The night that I was supposed to introduce my drawings to the world ended in a way no one could have predicted but the outpouring of support from strangers had captivated the news media.

A bystander brought to that street by the barrage of fire trucks had captured an image with their smartphone of my body sprawled across the hood of the police car. My name was front page news. The real reason the fireman were all on that street was shadowed by the story of the burgeoning artist who had walked into the path of a police car. No one cared that three utility workers had become trapped in the basement of that building when they were working on the gas line. The old and rotted floor above them had collapsed on them. Thankfully they were all pulled to safety and brought to the same hospital as me.

Within days of the accident, all of the drawings I had displayed at the gallery space were purchased by people I've never met. Zoe's husband, Beck, had taken it on himself to rummage through the box of drawings I kept hidden in my apartment. He'd framed many, taken them to the gallery and as quickly as he hung them, they sold.

As I recovered in a hospital bed surrounded by my parents, Zoe, Vanessa, and Dane, the dream I'd kept hidden within me, of being a recognized artist, had finally started to come true.

"Bridget." My mother steps closer and taps her fingers against my shoulder. "I need to talk to you."

When I'd told her and my father that I wanted to rest it was a thinly veiled attempt at garnering just a few minutes alone. My mother had made the unilateral decision to move in with me after I was released from the hospital. She's been staying in the second bedroom, although that's truly only when she's fast asleep. The rest of the time she's hovering and as much as I've needed and loved her help, it's time for her to go home. My father is here visiting this weekend and with any hope she'll be on the train with him when he leaves tonight.

"What is it?" I roll onto my right shoulder, taking care to keep my left hand out of harm's way. I've been wearing a cumbersome plaster cast since they set my wrist. I've become surprisingly adept at maneuvering my life around it.

"Your landlord was here earlier," she says as he pinches the bridge of her nose. It's a gesture I've seen countless times since I was a child. It's a physical sign of the emotional toll something is taking on her. I'm guessing that she's tiring of being my roomie as much as I am.

I push myself up so I'm resting on my right elbow. "What did he want?"

"Your lease is almost up." She leans her leg against the mattress. "I think you should move back to Connecticut with us."

I bite my lip to ward off the undeniable urge to list the myriad of reasons why that would be the worst possible decision of my life. I, instead, opt for logical over emotional. "I'm going to look for a new place this week. I can afford something better now."

"You can afford something better?" she parrots back as she sweeps her hand in the air. "This place is a dump and it costs a small fortune, Bridget. You can't afford to live in this city."

I actually can. I still have my job at the pub and even though I'm out of commission for the next few weeks, Elliott assured me, when he visited me last week with a bouquet of flowers in hand, that my job was there as soon as I was ready. Until then, the money that my drawings have brought in has given me a cushion in my savings account that I've never had before. "I'm staying here, mom. I don't want to go back."

"I've already talked to a friend back home and there's an available job for a program coordinator at a family center."

Not one word in her statement interests me in the least. I've long abandoned the notion that I'd use my degree to help others. If I do that, I'll be sacrificing my own happiness and goals. I'm finally starting to see some positive recognition for my work. Granted it might all be because I was run down by a police car, but it's not how you got there, it's more about what you do once you're there, right?

"I'm going to stay here and draw."

Her head darts to the left so she can look directly at me. I've seen the same look in her eyes before. When I was young I attributed it to her anger over the fact that I didn't complete my chores or I failed to get the grade she expected me to get on a test. Now that I'm older I see it for what it really is, concern. "Bridget, you barely know him."

It's a conversation leap that might have been disorienting if not for the fact that she's brought up my relationship with Dane at least twice a day since I was released from the hospital. He's visited almost daily and each time he's been nothing but courteous and kind to her. She, on the other hand, has taken her time warming up to him.

"I want to be an artist, mom," I say genuinely, making a conscious decision to keep Dane's name out of this. "I have to stay here to build on the interest in my work. This is a turning point for me."

"You can do that back at home." Her voice is breathless. "I'm worried about you."

I'm twenty-three-years-old. If I'm going to forge ahead with a future for myself it has to start with pushing her to let me go. "Trust me, mom. I'm doing what I need to do."

Her bottom lip trembles and just as she's about to sit on the edge of the bed, my father appears in the doorway. "Bridget will be fine. We'll come back next month to see her. It's time to go."

# TWO

"I thought she'd never leave." Dane's arms are around me as soon as I close the door to my apartment. "I like your mom, but the woman should get a job as a bodyguard. She never left us alone."

She hadn't. For the past three weeks my time with Dane has consisted of chaperoned visits in the living room of my place. My mother had grilled him with a barrage of questions about his youth, his family and his future career aspirations.

I'd intervened more than once to pull him from her overbearing clutches, but he'd held his own. He had answered each of her questions honestly. He'd assured her that he wasn't going to rush into anything with me and he'd actually pulled a smile onto her face when he brought her a blueberry bagel and a tea one morning after his shift. He had remembered her mentioning that a bakery on the Upper West Side made the best bagel she'd ever had and he went out of his way to hand deliver it. It was as much a surprise to me as it was to her.

"She's gone now." I scoop my casted arm behind his back. "I'm finally free."

He throws his head back in laughter and I glance up. Since the accident, his expression has volleyed between hope and concern. The night that I was hit, he had traveled in the ambulance with me to the hospital, holding tightly to my right hand. He had paced in the waiting room with my family and friends for word on my condition. Since then, he's come to visit me at least once a day. Even though the only intimacy we've shared the past few weeks has been hand holding and a few kisses, his presence has energized me in a way that nothing else could.

"How are you feeling?" He leans down to rest his forehead against mine. "Is your arm okay?"

I rub it gently over his back. "The doctor said I should have this thing removed in ten days and then I'll do some therapy. I'll be back to full strength in no time."

He shakes his head slightly. "You can't push it, Bridget. You have to let your body heal at the pace it wants to."

All my body really wants right now is to be nude in my bed with his. "I feel like the accident happened a lifetime ago. I have so many plans. I'm ready to get back out there."

"Not yet." His hands slide down my back to cup my jean covered ass. "Right now, you're not going anywhere. I've waited for weeks to get you alone."

"I'm all yours," I whisper as he glides his soft, supple lips over mine.

***

"I can't wait, Bridget." His breath flows over the back of my neck. "I want to taste you but I have to be inside of you."

I'm not going to say a thing. It's exactly what I want too. He'd carefully pulled the white t-shirt I had been wearing over my head before he knelt down to unzip my jeans and push them from my body. He'd taken not more than a minute longer to force my panties down. His lips had kissed a gentle path over my hip bone where a large bruise is finally fading. I'd heard his breath catch at the muted purple and yellow tones of it.

"I don't want to hurt you." His voice is low as his hands grip my waist. "Come and get on the bed. I want to see your face."

I let him take the lead, not because I'm not quaking from sheer want, but because I want to see his face too. I want to revel in the way his lips part when he's thrusting himself into me. I need to soak in the vision of his eyes closing when he feels me clenching around him as I find my release.

He holds my hand as he lowers me onto the bed. I watch in silence as he sheaths his thick cock in a condom. His labored breathing is the only sound in the space.

I move my legs as he drops his knee onto the mattress and I throw my left hand over my head when I feel his cock rub against my core.

"Bridget." My name flows from his lips within a muted moan as he grazes his long fingers over my folds. "You're so wet."

Each time he'd kissed me goodbye the past few weeks, my body had ached for him. I know that part of that is just the need that was borne from the intimate moments we've shared in this room before my accident, but there's more to it than that. When we're like this, on the cusp of sharing ourselves with one another, there's vulnerability within his eyes that I feel inside of me too. I've had lovers in the past that fulfilled me in a physical way but I've never connected with a man on any emotional level during sex. It's new for me, and as much as I crave the taste and feel of Dane's body, I want that emotional connection just as much.

"I want..." my voice trails as he leans back to draw the head of his cock over my clit.

"You want me to fuck you," he growls.

My legs fall open even more from the sheer weight of my body's need. I don't want to mask what I'm feeling. I just want him.

He inches forward, leans down to cover my mouth with his lips and pushes inside of me with one, painful, powerful stroke.

I lift my ass off the bed, bite his bottom lip and give in to the pleasure only this man can give me.

# THREE

"Do you want me to stop at the market on my way over tomorrow?" He walks back into my bedroom, his naked body on display. "All I could find was this apple and a few slices of bread."

He's exaggerating, but only slightly. My mother had gleefully handed her credit card information over to the market that's a block away once she realized that they delivered groceries. She's not wasteful though and so she had purchased only what we needed each day. This morning, her and my father had enjoyed a large brunch before they packed up some sandwiches for the train ride home. I guess when I told her I could take care of myself, she took it literally.

"No." I reach forward to take a small bite of the apple when he holds it out to me. "I'll go myself."

He takes a hearty bite of the fruit and smiles as he chews. "You're so independent."

It's a compliment that I'll greedily accept. I've always been independent and if I've learned anything from the accident, it's that I can take care of myself, even if my mother can't see it. I'd taken the time to listen intently when Vanessa instructed me on how to wrap the cast up before I showered each day. I'd dutifully done the exercises my doctor, Ben Foster, had shown me to help heal my ribs and I'd gotten an appointment with a physical therapist so that she could help me get back to my prime as quickly as possible.

"I've taken care of myself for a long time." I nod towards the apple and I'm rewarded with a smile and an outstretched hand. I take another bite.

"I like that about you. You don't expect anything from anyone."

It's the perfect segue into a discussion about the one subject we've been dodging around for the past few weeks. My mind hadn't been focused on anything but getting better so I hadn't even formed a thought about Maisy the first week or two after the accident. Since then I've brought it up twice and both times Dane has told me that he's handling it. In the broad range of the meaning of those words, I haven't found any comfort.

I expected him to invite me back to his place at some point just to escape the incessant questioning of my mother, but it hadn't happened. When I asked him about it last week, he told me his ex-girlfriend was still living in the house and that lawyers were hammering out the details.

As much as I want to believe that it will all be settled soon and Dane's life will no longer be bound in any way to Maisy's, the nagging voice of my mother is pulling on my doubts. I had confided in her, in a weak moment that he had lived with a woman in the past. She had quickly jumped into her role as my protector to warn me that lingering feelings can pull a man from the warmth of a new relationship back into a dark place if the woman he once loved is waiting there for him.

"I've been meaning to ask you about something…"

"I have to meet with my lawyer tomorrow." He interrupts as he tosses the apple's core into the wastebasket. "I can come over once I'm done with that."

"How's that going?" I pull the twisted sheet from the bed around my body. It's a feat better left for someone with two functioning hands, but I do my best. "You haven't said much about that."

He leans down and tugs his boxer briefs up his legs. The simple gesture suggests that he's feeling as protective of himself as I am. "There hasn't been anything to tell. She still refuses to leave."

Considering the fact that he told me that he purchased the house before she moved in, the law seems clear to me. I may not have hours of law school lectures to back me up, but I've watched enough courtroom dramas to know that he has more claim to the property than she does if his name is on the title documents, especially in New York where there aren't any clear laws in place regarding common law relationships. "Does she even have a case? I mean, aren't you the sole owner of your house?"

His left brow cocks as he swallows hard. There's a hesitation there that only fuels the fire of suspicion that has been brewing within me for weeks. "I do own it but she helped me with expenses. We lived there together."

I don't need the reminder. It's not that there's a spear of jealousy that darts through me when he mentions the depth of his connection with Maisy. I'm well aware that he loved her and the knowledge that they shared a home is evidence enough of their intention to have a future together. There's just a nagging voice in the back of my mind, which sounds a lot like my mother, telling me that there may be more to their relationship than he's let on.

"What will it take to settle things between you?" I ask not caring that the words sound pointed and brash. "Is she planning on moving out ever?"

His gaze falls to the floor and his shoulder surge forward. I hear the faint sound of a curse word beneath his breath. "She's going to move out. She has to."

Someone should probably tell Maisy that. I want to say that to him only because I sense that there's a small part of him that he's holding back from me. I can't pinpoint it and even though we've grown closer the past few weeks, I want his past to be just that. I don't want it to creep into our future and stall what is growing between us.

"Have you talked to Garrett about it?" I ask knowing it's a silly question. His cousin is a probate attorney so I'm not even sure he could offer any legal advice that would help Dane see the light at the end of the tunnel, but it's worth a suggestion.

"I did." He reaches down to pull on his jeans.

Nothing follows those words. He silently puts on the sweater he was wearing when he arrived before he pushes his feet into the black loafers he kicked off when he came into my bedroom.

If I learned anything that night when I was hit by the car it's that life is fleeting and everything can change in the blink of an eye. There's a question that has been sitting on the edge of my tongue since he first told me he'd left his girlfriend the night we met. If I don't ask him now, when we're immersed in this subject, and he's already headed out my apartment door, I may never find the courage again.

"Dane?"

He turns towards me as a brilliant smile courses across his lips. "Bridget."

I swallow hoping that the motion will dislodge the words from deep within me. I close my eyes briefly before I look directly into his eyes. "Did you ever think about marrying Maisy?"

He steps towards me and for the briefest moment I wonder if he's going to kiss me to try and quiet my need to understand about his past. He stops before he reaches the edge of the bed to look down at me. "I had a ring in my pocket at the restaurant. I was going to ask her to marry me the night I met you."

# FOUR

Trying to get dressed with both a broken arm and a reeling mind isn't an easy task. Add to that the fact that I'm still nursing tender ribs, and it's a disaster waiting to happen.

I struggle with my panties before Dane silently drops to his knee to help me. He reaches to grab my right hand, pulling it up to his lips for a light kiss on my palm before he places it on his shoulder. I hold onto him, balancing myself as I raise one foot off the floor, before I move the other so he can slide my panties on for me. He does the same with my jeans and as he carefully guides my casted hand through the arm hole of my t-shirt, he says my name in no more than a whisper.

"Her plan for the past year was for us to get engaged on her birthday."

The words feel foreign given what we just did and even though he's not talking in a raised tone, they feel and sound too loud for the small space. I brush past him, wanting to escape the sight of my bed where we've just made love.

"It was your birthday," I say quietly as I walk into the living room. "I met you on your birthday."

He shoves one of his hands into the front pocket of his jeans. "Her birthday was five months ago. I couldn't do it. I couldn't bring myself to ask her then."

I should take some comfort in those words but I can't. He may have put off the inevitable popping of the question along with the presentation of the token diamond ring for a few months, but he just told me not more than five minutes ago that he was prepared to propose the night before we first slept together. If I'm not the poster girl for rebounds right now, I should be.

"You were going to ask her to marry you?" I ask as much to hear the words from my own lips. "Why didn't you tell me that before?"

His eyes scan my face looking for something that I can't give to him right now. It's reassurance. He wants me to give him a sign that I understand but I don't. I can't. "I couldn't do it, Bridget. I couldn't ask her. I realized that night that it was over."

Call it cold feet if you will. Maybe it was engagement ring buyer's remorse but they were close enough for marriage to be part of the equation. He may have ran for the hills, or my bed, before he popped the question but the emotions that led him to the store where he bought the ring, and the desire to get dressed in a suit for the celebration of his birthday and planned engagement can't just disappear in the blink of an eye. "I don't know if I would have been with you..."

"What?"

I look up and into his face. His expression is unreadable. "I wouldn't have slept with you if I had known you were that close to getting married."

He rakes his hand through his messy brown hair. "Don't say that."

I rest my casted arm against my chest, suddenly feeling a dull ache in every part of my body. "I mean it. I didn't know it was that serious. I wouldn't have done it if I had known."

"I didn't want to be with her anymore." He heaves out a sharp breath. "I've moved on."

*In record time and apparently with the first woman he saw, who just happened to be me.*

I shouldn't be standing here judging his life choices but the fact that I'm one of them makes it unavoidable. The man moved effortlessly from a near engagement to being my lover all in the span of a day.

I smooth my hand over the cast before I look down at the floor. "I don't want to be your rebound, Dane. I don't want to be that."

"Bridget." His voice softens. "I checked out of my relationship with Maisy months before I met you. I was at the restaurant because I didn't want to hurt her but that night... the night of my birthday... I realized I was hurting us both too much by staying."

I see truth in his eyes but I can't tell if it's my desperate want to find it there or if it's genuine. "I like you, Dane. I like being with you but it's too soon. It's so soon."

"It's not." He leans down to brush his full lips against my forehead. "My heart has been empty for a long time, Bridget. I finally feel things again."

I don't say a thing. I only close my eyes as I feel his hands slide down to my shoulders before he pulls me into his chest to hold me there in the quiet silence of my apartment.

# FIVE

"Wait." Her hand flies into the air between us. "Just, wait."

I had to talk to someone and given the fact that my mother has been looking for an excuse to send me a one way ticket back to Connecticut and Vanessa's fiancé is related to Dane, my choices are limited.

I look at Vane first before I level my gaze back on Zoe's face. We're in Central Park. I had tried to sketch before they arrived but the muddled image of Dane dropping to his knee in Axel NY that night to ask a woman to marry him keeps clouding my thoughts. I may not know exactly what Maisy looks like but in my mind's eye, my focus is her left hand where an engagement ring almost found a permanent home.

"Zoe," I say her name in exasperation. I had barely given her time to sit on the bench next to me before I tore into a disjointed recounting of how I met Dane, how quickly I've fallen for him and his confession yesterday about almost asking his ex-girlfriend to marry him.

"Bridget," she interrupts before I can utter another word. "You're telling me that the night he met you, he was about to get engaged?"

Trying to twist the situation into something other than what it is, won't change a thing. "Yes. He had an engagement ring in his pocket when he took me home."

Her eyes drop from my face to where Vane is asleep in his stroller. She carefully adjusts the soft blue blanket that is covering his lap. "Remember the night Beck came into the pub? That first night we met him?"

It's hard to forget that night. I'd recognized Brighton Beck in an instant because of my admiration for his work. I'd fallen in love with his watercolor paintings when I saw them in an exhibit in a museum in Rhode Island during my sophomore year of college. I'd approached his table when I noticed him sitting in the pub. It was after he'd hit on one of the other servers. He'd muttered something inaudible about a woman he loved before he ordered a scotch. By the time I'd brought the drink to his table, he was eyeing up Zoe. It was obvious to everyone in the pub that he was there for two reasons. He needed to drink and he wanted to fuck. After spending ten minutes talking to her, he'd left alone.

"He was wasted, Zoe." I try to contain a small smile. "Remember how drunk he was?"

She laughs quietly. "He had a lot to drink that night. He was torn up about a girl."

"What girl?" My curiosity pushes the words out before I have time to think about masking them in something less direct. I've longed wondered about the woman he was muttering about that night but I've never felt comfortable asking Zoe. I wouldn't have known how to bring it up without reminding her of someone from his past who was obviously important to him.

She pulls on the corner of the stroller edging it closer to the bench. "Her name isn't important. She's not important anymore but on that first night when I met him, he said he loved her."

I know that my expression can't contain the utter shock I feel so I don't even try to curb it. "What?"

"It's so twisted." She scratches her left brow. "A woman he loved got married to someone else that day."

"She got married the day we met Beck?"

"A few hours before that," she says the words softly as she twists her fingers around her wedding rings.

I have so many questions but they're all running into one another in such a twisted mess that I can't vocalize even one of them. I just stare at the side of her face.

"He needed me right then." She turns to look at me. "If I would have shut him out because he was getting over someone else, I would have lost the love of my life."

I shake my head slightly as my eyes dart down to the sketchpad in my lap. "I understand what you're saying but that's you and Beck. You were made for each other."

"We were." She moves forward on the bench so she can brush her fingers softly over Vane's forehead. "Sometimes you meet the right person when you least expect it. You don't get to choose when love walks into your life, Bridget."

"I barely know him." I look off into the distance of the crowded park, hoping she won't see my scattered emotions. "I'm not in love with him."

"Don't close off your heart because you think you know what he needs." She taps my knee. "He's the only one who knows what he's feeling and from I saw right after your accident, he's crazy about you."

# SIX

"Do you know the name of the physical therapist you'll be working with?"

"I have it written down." I gesture towards my kitchen table. "I keep everything in a pile over there so when I need something I know where to find it."

Dane glances briefly towards the papers before he looks back down at me. "Did Ben recommend someone or were you assigned someone after you left the hospital?"

It had only taken me a few days to realize that Dane had more than a passing acquaintance with the doctor who took care of me when I was rushed to the ER. Ben Foster is the kind of physician who puts everything he has into his work. He'd explained as thoroughly as he could in layman terms, the extent of my injuries, to my parents and me. He'd never rushed me through an examination and he answered each and every one of my questions.

On the day I was being discharged, he had personally sat next to me and gone through the protocol I needed to follow after my release. He'd called to arrange my physical therapy himself and as I left the hospital, I knew that the care I'd received had helped me immeasurably. I got home with a renewed sense of purpose and a strong belief that I'd fully recover in time.

I adjust myself slightly on the cramped couch. Dane had pulled me into his lap when he arrived and even with all the doubts still floating in my mind, I'd nuzzled my cheek into his chest. "Dr. Foster arranged it."

"You should call him Ben." He leans down to graze his lips across my cheek. "He's my friend. He told you to call him Ben, didn't he?"

He had. I can't recall our first meeting because I was still in shock but the next day I vaguely remember him introducing himself to my parents as Ben. "How long have you known him?"

"I don't know." His chest rumbles as he chuckles deeply. "Maybe a year, but it could be more."

The exact timing of the friendship doesn't matter. I don't care if they've known each other forever or for a month. I do care that he clearly wants me on a first name basis with someone he views as important to him. That has to count for something.

"I've been thinking about what we talked about the last time I was here." His index finger catches my chin to jerk it upwards until our eyes are locked.

Unless he's referring to the lack of fresh produce in my kitchen, I know exactly where this discussion is headed. Just to be sure, I'm going to get behind the driver's wheel and steer it in the direction I want. "You mean when you told me about Maisy?"

His expression does nothing to hide the fact that my blunt words stun him. He pushes his back into the couch just a touch but it's enough that he has to shift my weight on his lap. "Yes."

Now that I have confirmation I realize that I don't know what I'm supposed to say next. Zoe's confession about Beck's feelings for another woman blazes across my thoughts. I want to give Dane the benefit of the doubt but I refuse to get pulled into a love triangle when I'm on the cusp of a breakthrough in my art career. I love spending time with him but I'm not going to forsake my entire future for a relationship that may crash and burn once he realizes that wedded bliss with Maisy is actually exactly what he wants. I can't risk derailing myself emotionally that way. It would impact me too much.

"I know that I should have been more open about how serious things were between me and her." His fingers slide over the leg of my jeans. "I was going to tell you that first night when we were drinking coffee in your kitchen, but I couldn't. I was worried that you wouldn't want to see me again."

If anything, the man has a grip on logic that is unwavering. He's right in thinking I likely wouldn't have let him back into my place the next night if I'd have known that he broke up with someone he cared that much about right before he rescued me from Larry's sweaty grasp.

"I want you to understand something." He pushes my left hand into my lap, stroking his fingers over the plaster cast. "I feel like I woke up that night. When I looked at Maisy sitting across the table from me, I didn't see my future anymore. I just saw my past."

I stare at my hand, wiggling my fingers the way Ben instructed me to do a few times each day. "Why did you wait until then to end it?"

"Exactly a year ago on that same night...on my birthday," he begins before he pushes a lock of hair behind my ear. "The night of my twenty-eighth birthday, Maisy told me she wanted to marry me."

I stare at his face. I see nothing but honesty in his eyes but it's impossible for me to judge whether that's based in reality or in my need to trust in everything that he says. "What did you say to her?"

"I can't remember." His finger slides down to my neck. "I remember exactly how I felt, but I can't remember saying anything to her after she told me she wanted to get married."

I ask the obvious because it's right there waiting for me. "How did you feel?"

"I felt panicked. I was scared."

I study the strength in his jawline. I soak in his chiseled features. After seeing him in his firefighter gear the night I was hit, I'd never label him as anything but strong and courageous.

"I should have ended it a year ago," he says the words softly. "I had to end it now or it would have only hurt her more."

I don't know Maisy but judging by the fragmented parts of her relationship that I'm hearing about, she had to have been in pain after the break up. She expected a proposal that night and instead her dreams of a happily-ever-after collapsed in the blink of an eye. That explains, at least partially, why she's still holding onto the house. It's the place where she built her plans for the future.

"I wish I had met you first, Bridget," he whispers the words against the skin of my neck. "I wish every day that you had walked into my life before I ever met her."

# SEVEN

I lean my cheek against the headboard as he lashes his tongue over my core again and again. "Dane, please."

The only response is a growl through the moans that have been pouring from his lips since he undressed us both and got on his back on my bed. He'd gently guided me onto his face and now, after coming already once, I'm too tender. I'm so close to another orgasm that I can already feel the rush flowing through me.

I grip tightly to the top of the headboard as I glide myself over his lips. His hands jump up to my thighs to hold me in place. I cry out from the high, knowing that as soon as I crash back down, he'll pull me back and onto his hard cock.

He licks me softly as I feel my body collapse beneath the weight of the pleasure. I try to move to gain distance only because it all feels like too much and if he dives back into my wetness full force, I'm going to pass right out. I already feel faint.

"I can't," I whisper as I look down at his eyes. "You need to stop."

He grazes his tongue slowly over the length of my cleft before he pushes my body back onto his chest. "I could eat you all night, Bridget. I love doing that."

I love when he does that too. "It feels so good."

I inch myself downwards as gracefully as I can but having my arm encased in a plaster prison doesn't help. I wince when I feel a burst of pain shoot through my side as I try and twist slightly to gain enough leverage to slide down to his stomach.

His hands land on my waist before I can react and I'm suddenly on my back with him hovering above me. "I'm sorry. I hurt you, didn't I?"

I look up into his handsome face. He'd shaved before he arrived at my apartment and each time he does that I'm taken back by how gorgeous and strong his face is. I doubt that he's ever looked in the mirror and questioned whether or not he's attractive. "You didn't."

"Why are you looking at me like that?" A small smile tugs at the corner of his lips. "You've never looked at me like that before."

I part my lips and dart my tongue over them. "I've never known anyone like you before."

"A fireman?"

I smile at the jest in his tone. "I don't know any firemen but that's not what I meant."

"What did you mean then?" He brings his hand to my forehead to softly brush away some wayward strands of hair.

"Sometimes I think you're too good to be true."

"I think the same thing when I look at you." His lips follow the path that his fingers just took. "I didn't know a woman like you was out there."

"I like when we're together," I confess softly knowing that revealing everything I'm feeling too soon, and when things are still unresolved between him and Maisy, isn't my best move but I can't help it.

He slides his lips over my cheek before he brushes them against mine. "I love when we're together."

I don't need more than that right now. It's enough to quiet the raging voices within me that are telling me that I shouldn't invest myself in this so soon. I'm trying not to but every moment I spend with him is making it harder and harder to stay objective.

He kisses me one more time, before he slides his body from the bed, reaches into the drawer of the nightstand and pulls a condom out.

***

"I wanted to ask you something." His breath is on my cheek.

I try to open my eyes but I'm exhausted.

After he'd sheathed himself, he'd sat on my bed with his back resting against the headboard. He'd helped me get onto his lap and then I'd ridden him until I'd come hard with my lips pressed against his.

The moment my body stopped shaking, he'd pushed me onto my back and he mounted me. He'd pulled my legs up against his chest and had thrust himself into me over and over again until he released with a deep growl pulled between the syllables of my name.

The look of raw pleasure on his face had brought me back to the brink and he'd lowered his hand to my core to gently glide his fingers over my flesh until I shuddered under the weight of one last intense climax.

"Bridget." His lips are on my neck. "Please look at me."

It's a request that I can't resist, regardless of how weary my eyelids feel. I pull them open slowly and I'm instantly greeted with the vision of his face only inches from mine. "What is it?"

He pulls the pad of his thumb over my bottom lip. "Can I stay here tonight? I want to sleep with you."

I want that too. I know, for a fact, that if he hadn't wakened me that I would have curled into the warmth and comfort of his side the moment he crawled under the covers with me. I have no doubt that I wouldn't have woken until the sunlight had poured into my room in the morning.

"Stay," I whisper into his chest as he tugs me into his body. "I want you to stay."

He adjusts himself next to me, pulls my casted arm onto his chest and rests his lips against my cheek as we both drift off to sleep.

# EIGHT

"I have a confession to make."

I've just walked back into my bedroom after brushing my teeth and my hair. Dane had insisted on having a shower even though he knew that the water at this time of the day would be as warm as the icy depths of the Arctic Ocean. I had giggled when I first walked into the bathroom and saw my toothbrush with toothpaste already on it. He'd done that for me before he gotten into the shower, turned on the water and let out a loud yelp.

I know that the next logical thing for me to ask is what the confession is but if it involves Maisy it's going to tarnish the memory of our first night actually sleeping together. He'd stayed over before but those nights were filled with passion and neither of us had slept more than a half hour at a time. Last night we fell asleep just before midnight and didn't wake until almost seven. It's a milestone and in my life, it's a rarity.

"It's about your drawing," he begins before he pulls on his boxer briefs. "It's actually about the drawing you did of me."

I had promised Dane that he could have the drawing before I'd hung it on the gallery wall. After news broke of my accident, people had flooded the gallery looking for my work. It was a community gesture meant to help raise funds for my recovery and the outpouring had been more than I ever imagined it would be. With the shock in getting over the accident, and the awe in knowing that my name was now associated with the word '*artist*,' I hadn't thought to tell anyone to put the drawing of Dane aside.

Once I realized that someone had purchased it, I felt instant regret but I decided right then, on the spot, that I'd draw him again as soon as I felt well enough to.

"Someone bought it," I say softly, not wanting to give credence to the words. It bites just to think about it, but it's even more painful to have to acknowledge it verbally. This is the first time we've spoken about it since that night.

"I bought it."

"What?" My eyes dart up to meet his. "You bought that drawing?"

He scratches the back of his neck. "I went back the next day. I waited until I knew you were okay and then I went to the gallery."

My intention from the moment I first brought my pencil to the paper to capture his handsome face was to give him the drawing. It would have been the first time I had given any of my work away. "I wanted to give it to you."

"I know." He reaches down to pull on his jeans. "I wanted it so badly that I went to get it."

The words hit me with an emotional force that's completely unexpected. That drawing represented so many things to me and it wasn't until I thought a stranger had taken it home, that I fully realized that.

It's not just the fact that it's the first time I've ever drawn someone I care for. It was more about that the drawing symbolized a shift in my life. It was a tangible reflection of my decision to share my work with the world. Dane had pushed me to do that, and within the penciled lines of his brow and the shading of his hairline, I'd captured the face of the person who held more belief in me than I held in myself.

Knowing that it meant so much to him that he went back to get it before it was lost forever, touches me on a level that feels too deep given the fact that we're still treading the waters of our new connection.

"I can't believe you bought it."

He tugs the sweater he was wearing when he arrived at my apartment yesterday back over his head. The static it generates, pulls his hair up and into a twisted mess. He looks even more striking when he's completely disheveled like this.

"I had to have it." He rakes his hand through his hair but it does little to calm it. "I just had to."

When I needed to make a decision on pricing the drawings, Brighton had urged me to consider the value in them. I had wanted to keep them at a reasonable price and to me that wasn't more than what amounted to a few cups of coffee. He had scolded me on not seeing the uniqueness in my own work. I'd given in when he suggested a few hundred dollars for each framed piece. I never expected Dane to pay that much, or anything.

"Let me give you back what you paid," I say it quickly. The words feel awkward and misplaced given the fact that he just told me that he invested what amounts to a good portion of his weekly pay on a drawing that was his to begin with.

"No." He reaches out to grab my elbow as I brush past him on my way to my purse. "It's worth way more than what I paid for it."

I giggle as I turn to look at him. "I wanted to give it to you."

"It's an investment." He leans down until his gaze is level with mine. "I see it as an investment."

I may not be an expert on romance, but I do know enough to recognize that there's nothing endearing in a man buying something as a financial investment. "An investment?"

He steeples his fingers together as he holds them in front of his lips. "Bridget."

I can't take anything from the simple tone of his voice. "What?"

"You invested yourself in that drawing," he begins before he rests his forehead against mine. "I'm investing myself in you. That drawing symbolizes something to me. It's a new beginning."

I reach up to cup his cheek in my palm. "I'm investing myself in you too."

"You don't know how seriously I take that." He brushes his lips against mine. "You are my future. I see it. I know it."

# NINE

"I received the report from Dr. Foster." She skims through the stack of papers that are attached to the clipboard in her hand. "He says that you're recovering nicely."

He would say that. I'm not sure the man knows how to be impolite to anyone. When I saw him this morning after Dane and I said goodbye in front of the hospital, Ben had removed the cast before he examined my pale, shriveled wrist. He was hopeful and told me that I'd done everything by the book, which meant that soon I'd regain most of the strength in my left arm.

When he'd tenderly touched my side, I had grimaced slightly from the faint bite of pain that still lingers. He'd warned me to avoid marathons which only spurred me on to make a joke about taking too many taxis around the city, and when he finally told me I was free to go, I'd thanked him for taking such good care of me.

He winked and told me that according to Dane, I was capable of taking care of myself. I smiled at the reminder of how he values my independence before I'd left the hospital and taken the subway to the rehabilitation center.

"Bridget?"

I turn to look at the woman assigned to help me over this last hurdle in my recovery. "Yes?"

"My name is Harper."

"It's nice to meet you." I study her face. She's not much older than I am, but the air in which she carries herself makes it feel as though she has an entire decade of life experience on me. Her hair is black and cut in a short bob that skims her defined jawline. Her eyes are a striking shade of green. She's exotic looking and even though she's dressed in scrubs, I feel as though I pale in her shadow. She'd be perfect for..." I'd like to draw you."

"What?" Her lips part slightly in an even smile. "Did you just say you want to draw me?"

I glance at the papers in her hand before I catch her gaze again. This will be the first time I say it to anyone. "I'm an artist."

"You're an artist?" She grins wildly, revealing a set of perfectly straight, white teeth. "I love art."

It's a broad statement but one I understand completely. I've been enamored with art, in its many forms, since I was a child. It's rare to meet someone who instantly brightens at the mention of it. "I do pencil portraits."

"Wait." Her hand leaps to my forearm. "Are you the girl who was hit by the police car?"

It's a label I'm hoping won't chase after me for my entire life but it's understandable that she'd make the association given the fact that I'm in her office with the intent of healing my broken wrist and I just told her I do pencil drawings. Images of my work had been splattered across the papers and the news sites online in the days following the accident.

"It is you." Her hand drops to her side. "I recognize you from the picture."

I'm not even going to ask if it she's making that connection based on that unforgiving image of me on the hood of the police car with my dress twisted around my thighs and my head nestled in a bed of broken glass.

"It's me," I confess. "I think you'd be perfect to draw."

"I'm honored that you'd ask me." The tone of her voice doesn't match the sentiment of the words. The fact that she takes a full step back only adds to my suspicions that the idea is making her completely uncomfortable.

"I wouldn't sell it if you're not okay with that," I try to reel her back in. "I just think your face captures so much. It has a story to tell."

Her gaze drops to the floor and for just an instant, I see her shoulders tremble. "I'll think about it."

I don't press for more than that. There are obvious secrets that she wants to keep hidden within herself and I'm not about to push this stranger to give me anything beyond the advice I need to get better. "What do I need to do for my wrist?"

Her entire body shifts with relief once she realizes I've changed the subject. Her index finger slides over the edge of the stack of papers. "I'll show you some light exercises you can do at home and then you'll come back in a few days. I'll evaluate your progress and we'll work our way up to more."

I nod in silence. I'll do whatever she needs me to do. I want to get back to work at the pub so I can move my life forward. I'm ready and as soon as my arm is completely healed, I'll be able to do it.

# TEN

"There's a vacancy here in our building." Zoe fumbles in her purse. "I have the mailbox key in here somewhere. I can't find it."

I hold out my hands because we've run through this exact scenario before. She doesn't pull her gaze from the depths of her oversized handbag as she starts handing things to me including a package of tissues, a baby bottle, a tube of lipstick and a silver bracelet.

"What don't you have in there?" I peer into the bag.

"My mailbox key."

I laugh as I pull the items closer to me. Harper told me I could use my left hand but not to carry anything that had much weight to it. I try to balance all the items Zoe handed to me against my chest.

"Oh shit." Her eyes dart up to my hands. "You don't have a cast anymore. You can't hold all of that."

I shake my head in protest. I want her to see that I'm doing just fine but she scoops it all back into her bag in a single, swift movement. "Now you're never going to find the key."

"Beck can get the mail when he comes home." She motions towards the expansive lobby. "Do you want me to see if the super can show you the vacant apartment?"

Zoe is caring and kind and at moments like this I can't help but label her as naïve. I have no idea about the financial logistics of her marriage to Beck. I know that once they fell in love with each other, that she had moved into his penthouse apartment. The fact that it has a Park Avenue address means that regardless of how many drawings I might sell this year, I doubt that I'd be able to rent a foot square space in the lobby to stand on. There's no way in hell I can afford to live within a twenty block radius of this place.

"I have my eye on a place in Murray Hill."

"Are you going to have a roommate?"

I shake my head slightly as I wave to the doorman who just nodded at us. "I can live there alone. The rent is reasonable. It's a sublet."

"Is it better than where you're living now?"

Considering the fact that Zoe used to be my roommate, I'd think she'd have held onto some fond memories of the place I live in. It may not be much to look at but it was my refuge when I arrived in Manhattan and it gave me a quiet and safe place to retire to when the city felt too big and overbearing for me.

"You used to live there too, Zoe," I point out as I fall in step beside her.

She pushes the call button for the elevator. "I miss it sometimes. I love my life now but I miss us hanging out the way we used to."

"You can come to my new place as soon as I move in," I offer as I follow her into the elevator. "I'll have you over for dinner."

"I'll bring the wine."

"You'll drink the wine," I tease.

"Can you feel it, Bridge?" She turns her head to the left to look right at me.

"Feel what?"

"You're on the cusp of great things." Her eyes dart up to follow the lighted pattern of the numbers as we race upwards. "Your life is about to change."

I do feel it and I couldn't be happier.

***

"What's going on with that woman?"

I know who she means. She's talking about Maisy.

When I agreed to come over to Zoe's place for lunch today it was with the sole intention of talking about my upcoming appearance on one of the local news shows. A reporter had left a message at the gallery yesterday, asking me to call him. I had and he wanted to do a human interest piece on me that included details about my life before the accident and my plans now that my drawings had grabbed the attention of so many people. I was both flattered and terrified by the proposition but when I'd called Zoe to run the idea past her, she'd insisted I call the reporter back and agree to the piece. She told me that any publicity would help my quest to further my career. I know she's right but I'm here for not only a sandwich, but also a pep talk on the side.

"What woman?" I ask knowing that it's only going to stall the inevitable for a few seconds.

"Maisy." She turns on her heel to face me. "That's the name of the woman your boyfriend almost married, right?"

*Way to push the knife into my heart and twist it twice, Zoe.*

I should correct her about the boyfriend part, but I don't. "There's nothing going on with her."

"Is he still living out of a suitcase?"

It's as if Zoe has sucked up all the worried energy from my mother and is now shooting it off in one hurried barb after another. "He's still figuring out his house stuff."

"It shouldn't take this long." She glances towards the hallway. "I asked around at the law office where I'm doing some intern work and everyone thinks it should have been settled by now especially since he owned the house himself."

I can't say that I'm shocked that she dragged my personal business into her workplace. It's all coming from a place of wanting to help but it makes me feel exposed and embarrassed. "I wish you wouldn't tell other people about my life."

"I worry about you." She turns back towards the counter and all the ingredients she pulled from the refrigerator. "Do you want lettuce on your sandwich?"

"I want you to trust that I know what I'm doing."

"Bridget," she begins before she lowers the jar of mustard in her hand onto the counter. "I saw with my own two eyes how much he cares about you. He was torn to shreds in the waiting room that night but his last relationship isn't settled yet. I just want you to be careful."

I stare at her back willing her to turn so I can look at her face but she doesn't budge. "I'm being careful, Zoe. I know what I'm doing."

"I hope you do. Your body just went through hell. Don't let him hurt your heart."

I don't respond. I can't find the words to tell her that I'm being as careful as I can be but I'm feeling things I've never felt before.

# ELEVEN

"You're going to be on television?" Dane's dark eyes sweep over my face. "That's amazing."

It's more terrifying than amazing, but I'll do what I've been doing all week. I'll fake it until I make it, or in my case, I'll pretend to be totally fine with the prospect of standing in the gallery being interviewed for one of the local morning shows, even though I'm doubting whether I'll be able to pull it off.

I skim my hand over my forehead. "Can you still see all those cuts that were on my head?"

He pushes the empty plate in front of him aside as he leans forward to rest his elbows on the table. "You're beautiful. There's not a mark on your face."

He's not the best person to ask how I look since he's so biased. When I'd arrived at this Italian restaurant, my hair was drenched, along with most of my body, from the torrential downpour. I had thought about grabbing an umbrella before I left my apartment to stop by the pub to talk to Elliott, but since my hand still isn't as strong as I need it to be, I'd decided that I'd tempt fate and venture into the outdoors with little more than a light sweater and hope. I should have taken the weather forecast more seriously. I guess when they say there's a ninety percent chance of rain, they actually mean it.

"This is a really important interview." I tap my foot against the tiled floor. "I want to showcase my work."

"Your work speaks for itself." He shifts his body so his back is now resting against the wooden chair. "I told you that people would love it."

He had told me that and it's one of the reasons why I'm about to go home to choose more images to frame for the gallery. Mrs. Boudreau called me earlier to tell me that two had been sold just today. As excited as I am to pick up the commission check she has waiting for me, I'm just as thrilled to know that my drawings are now hanging in someone's home or office.

"I'm still shocked at how well they're selling," I say truthfully as I push the fork in my hand on the edge of a piece of pasta in the bowl in front of me. "I'm going to get more exposure when I do the news piece."

"Is it just about your drawings?" He picks up the glass of red wine he ordered when he arrived. He's been nursing it slowly throughout our dinner. I finished my glass even before my entrée arrived. My nerves over the interview had craved the taste of it and before I knew it, I was feeling slightly light headed, but no less anxious.

I cup the fingers of my left hand in my right. "The reporter wants to talk about the night of the accident too."

"Are you okay with that?"

I hadn't considered the question until now. When I first had to face my parents after being hit by the police car, I'd been overcome with raw emotion. I understood the gravity of what had happened to me. I know that if the police officer hadn't slowed when he did, that I might have suffered life changing injuries, or worse. I get that.

Since that night, I've challenged myself to accept that I've been given a second chance. It may not appear that way to the people around me, but I'm stronger now than when I stepped off that curb. I can talk about it. I can recount it and I can honestly tell the reporter that my life has changed since that night.

"I'm fine with talking about it." I am and I don't want Dane to view me as a wounded bird who has yet to find her wings again. I'm back on track and now that I'm going to therapy, I'm going to be back working at the pub soon. Once that happens I can tuck away all the money I'm making on my drawings into my rainy day fund.

"Bridget," he says my name slowly before there's a thoughtful pause while he studies my face. "They're bound to ask why you were on the street. It was blocked off that night."

Everyone is bound to ask that and they have. I've always answered honestly which meant telling my parents, Zoe and even the doctors at the hospital that I was running towards a man I'd been seeing.

"I wanted to see you," I murmur, begrudgingly admitting that my overwhelming need to embrace him on the street that night had landed me in the ER.

His eyes drop to his lap and I feel bereft from the lack of a smile. He doesn't say anything at all.

"Dane?" I tap my right hand against the edge of the table. "What is it?"

He shakes his head only slightly and if I had blinked in that second, I would have missed the motion. "I feel guilty. It tears me up inside that you got hurt because of me."

"I got hurt because of me." I extend my right hand across the table. "I'm the one who stepped out onto the street."

"I've never felt as scared in my life, Bridget, as when I saw that car." He reaches for my hand, pulling it into his. "I just wanted to protect you."

I glance down at our hands, marveling in the way mine fits so perfectly in his. "We can protect each other. I'll help you and you can help me."

"Deal," he says quietly as he leans forward to glide his lips over my palm.

I smile at the sweet gesture even though inside I'm wondering if he's already protecting me from his past and the inevitable consequences it's going to have on our future.

# TWELVE

"I took some ribbing at work after the accident." He shakes the rain from the umbrella he'd held over our heads as we walked back to my apartment after dinner.

I slide my wet sweater off my shoulders before I kick off my flats. "What do you mean?"

He rests the umbrella's handle against the door of my apartment and then he slips his own shoes off. "The guys at the station tease me about not saving my girlfriend."

My heart stutters at the mention of the word '*girlfriend*' so I labor on, trying to find some words that won't sound like the mottled mess my emotions are right now. "You're not a superhero."

His hands are around my waist before I can react. "I'm not a superhero? Is that what you just said?"

I giggle at the playful tone of his deep voice. "You think you are but you're not."

"I might be." He spins me around quickly. "I would have jumped in front of that car to save you, Bridget."

I swallow hard from the palpable emotion in his voice. "You tried to help. I saw you running."

He presses his lips to my forehead. "I wasn't fast enough. I can't outrun a speeding car."

"That's true but it was a valiant effort," I say through a half-smile.

He slides his hands down my body to the bottom of the simple blue blouse I'm wearing. "Lift your arms up."

I do, not just because I love the authoritative bite that sometimes takes over his voice, but because I'm freezing and every inch of my skin is damp. I watch his expression as he unclasps the front of my bra before lowering himself to his knees to rid me of my wet jeans.

"Your body is so beautiful." He brushes his moist lips across my stomach. "Have I told you how beautiful I think you are?"

He has. He says those words to me almost every time I see him. I doubt that I'd ever tire of it. It was the first thing he said to me the morning after my accident when he came to my hospital room to see me. I'd cried then, not because the words were so meaningful but because I saw one lone tear in his eye. We've never talked about it, but it's a memory I'll carry with me forever.

"You tell me all the time." I shiver from the chill in the air.

He pulls me close. "We can take a hot shower to warm up."

"I'd like that." I snuggle into his chest, knowing that it's a prelude to the pleasure he's going to give to me later tonight.

"Come with me." He wraps his arm over my shoulder as he guides us both down the hallway of my apartment to the bathroom and the warmth that waits.

***

His jaw tightens as he absorbs what I just asked him. He doesn't respond so I repeat the question.

"I asked if you have a picture of Maisy."

He ignores me again in favor of pushing his cheek into the pillow next to mine. I'd studied his face in the shower while he washed my hair and carefully soaped my body before rinsing me under the warm water.

I'd let him brush out my hair while he talked about a fire he had been called to a few days ago in Brooklyn. The excitement in his voice was a window into why he's a fire fighter. His breathing quickened and his cheeks flushed when he told me about the family who had lived in the townhouse and how they had escaped with just the clothing on their backs.

It's a job that I can't imagine wanting to go to each day. The destruction and inevitable death that he must be witness to has to bear down on a person over time, much the same way being a doctor or police officer does. I couldn't do it. My emotional fortitude would give out under the weight of the dark parts of the job.

"Do you have a picture of your last boyfriend?" he counters with an underlying anger woven into the tone.

I'm not about to be bullied by a man who told me, when we were walking back to my apartment, that he was going to fuck me senseless. "No, I don't. I deleted every picture of him."

"Why don't you ever talk about him?"

It's a fair tactic but it's not going to deter me from the subject at hand. "He's part of my past. There's nothing left between us."

I know the words are a veiled jab at the fact that he's still immersed in a legal battle with Maisy. I watched the way his expression shifted from happy to sullen when a text message came in on his phone right when we walked back into my bedroom. It might have been her, or it could have been from someone else, but it shifted his mood in such an abrupt way that he pulled an obvious fake yawn from somewhere within him and told me that he was too tired to make love.

I'm not asking about her as a means to punish him for denying me pleasure. I'm asking because I'm tired of feeling as though I'm being kept in the dark about an integral part of his past.

"I don't have a picture of her." He slides his body up so he's resting on his right arm. "I thought you understood about Maisy."

"Before the accident," I say as I sit up in the bed. "That night... the night of the accident, you said that you were meeting with her to iron things out. That was weeks ago."

"I was called to work half-way through that meeting." He scrubs his hand over his forehead. "She hasn't been willing to talk to me since."

"What if she never talks to you?" I ask out of a desperate need to understand. "This could go on for years."

"Sooner or later I'll have to let it go..." his voice trails. "I'll just have to walk away and lose my house."

"I don't understand." I swallow hard hoping that it will help me broach a subject I haven't brought up to this point. "I know that in New York State that there are no laws in place in common law relationships. How does Maisy have a claim on your house?"

"How would you know that?" I can not only hear the defensive tone in his voice, I see it in his face.

"My friend is studying to be a lawyer," I say quietly even though Zoe wasn't the one who told me about the law. I'd researched it myself online. "We talked about it the other day."

I stall my breathing waiting for him to launch to his feet but he doesn't. He closes his eyes briefly before he reaches to touch my cheek. "It's a complicated situation, Bridget. I don't love her anymore but I can't throw her out on the street. I just want it to be over so I can move back in and get on with my life."

It's a gallant statement that fits exactly with who he is. "Do you think she's taking advantage? Is she staying because she hopes you'll give in and go back to her?"

"It honestly doesn't matter why she's doing it." He drops his hand onto the sheet. "If I have to walk away and give it to her, I will. It's just a house. It's not everything to me."

With that, he skims his lips over mine, turns over and falls asleep.

# THIRTEEN

"You were amazing, Bridget." Tex Henderson pats me on the back. The man is old enough to be my father and I doubt that he cares an ounce about my drawings, but when the cameras were rolling, he was my biggest supporter. He pointed out the detail in my portraits and he enthusiastically insisted that people come down to the gallery to purchase my work to support an up and coming artist.

I smile softly as I glance back at my drawings hung on the wall. "When will the segment air?"

He nods towards the cameraman he brought with him. "It looks like that will happen on Friday. It'll be in the second hour, so around half past eight. I'll text you the exact time so you don't miss it."

"That would be great."

He plucks a wayward piece of lint off his grey suit jacket. "I didn't bring it up on camera, but is there any litigation between you and the NYPD?"

Garrett, Vanessa's fiancé, had asked me about this very subject a few days after my accident. It wasn't that he thought I could pursue a civil lawsuit against the police department or the officer driving the car that hit me. He wanted to explain to me that since I had walked past a barrier and stepped onto a blocked street that I'd be facing years of expensive legal fees if I launched a suit against them. It was never my intention. I know that I was wrong and according to Garrett, I'm lucky that they didn't arrest me for failing to stay behind the police tape.

"There's nothing like that," I answer honestly. "I'm just grateful that I'm getting better."

"This has been pretty incredible, hasn't it?" He tips his chin in the direction of my portraits. "You've become an overnight sensation."

I wouldn't go that far. More than half of the drawings I kept in the box under my bed have sold since the accident, and I'm still hoping to sell more before my story becomes one of the hundreds that becomes forgotten when a new, fresh tale takes its place.

"Are you working on any new portraits?"

I glance up at his face as he asks the question. "I'm hoping to start back this week."

He gazes past me to the door of the gallery where the cameraman just exited. "I have a question but let's keep it between us, okay?"

I take a half-step back when I realize that we're the only two people left in the space. Mrs. Boudreau had run out under the guise of getting something for lunch when the camera arrived. I can tell, just by the few times I've been in her presence, that unless she's donning full make-up and styled hair, she doesn't want to be within shooting distance of any camera.

I twist my fingers together as I look towards the door. "What's the question?"

"Can I commission one of these?" He brushes past me and points at one of the framed images of a woman I drew last year outside a laundromat on the Lower East Side.

"What do you mean?"

"My wife is an angel." He taps his hand against his chest. "She's put up with me for thirty years. Can you draw her for me?"

It's the first time I've ever been asked to capture someone's loved one in my sketchpad. I've always just ventured out of my apartment with an open mind and pencil in hand. I've let my imagination and curiosity guide me. "I've never done that before."

"Are you willing to? I'll obviously pay you for the trouble."

I pull on the long silver necklace hanging around my neck, before I adjust the front of the black dress I'm wearing. "I'd be happy to. I'd love to do that for you."

"I'll call you to set it all up," he says as he takes a measured step towards the door. "You're a special girl, Bridget. I'm glad you pulled through."

It's too dramatic given the fact that anyone passing me on the street wouldn't know that I'd been hit by a car. "Thank you but I wasn't that seriously injured."

"My daughter was killed by a drunk driver." He only turns slightly towards me. "She would have been your age."

There are no words to capture what I should say to him. "I'm sorry."

"Don't waste your second chance." He holds his phone in the air. "I'll call you next week to set up a time to talk about the drawing."

I only nod as I watch him walk out of the door and into the pedestrian traffic on the crowded SoHo sidewalk.

# FOURTEEN

"I thought about the drawing." Harper tentatively touches my wrist. "I've actually been thinking about it since you brought it up."

That was more than two weeks ago. Since then, I've been back to see her three times and I haven't broached the subject again. I saw the hesitation in her eyes, and even though I know her portrait would be stunning, it's not my place to pester her just to fuel my creative need.

"Does this hurt?" She pushes on the top of my wrist.

I shake my head. "No. There's a bit of discomfort but it's not pain."

Her brow furrows slightly. "Did you follow all the instructions I gave you? Have you been doing those exercises I showed you the last time you were here?"

I have been doing everything she's told me to do, religiously. I've been mindful of the fact that I can't pick up anything too heavy with my left hand yet so I'm still juggling my purse, my sketchpad and any groceries I pick up on my way home in my right arm. "I've done it all."

"You're a dream patient, Bridget."

I smile at the compliment. It's not that I need any reassurance from her that my arm is getting better. I feel it myself. It's not only providing me with a sense of accomplishment, but it's also helping to heal the emotional wounds of that night. I haven't given in to the need I feel to cry. I have yet to do that. Each time I go online and see that image of myself sprawled over the hood of the police car, with my eyes closed, I feel my emotions cresting. I push them back down. It's not because I'm afraid to acknowledge them. I know that I need to. It's more that the picture represents what might have been and I'm grateful for every moment that I now have to pursue my goals.

"What should I be doing this week?" I stare down at my wrist. "Do I just keep up with the same exercises?"

"For now I'd advise that." She jots something down on a piece of paper. "Next week I think we'll graduate to some free weights to build up strength."

"I can't wait," I say with a genuine smile. "I'm pretty sure my right bicep is huge since I carry everything in that arm."

She tosses her head back in laugher. "We'll even that out."

"Let's talk about the drawing." I push the arm of my sweater back down so it covers my wrist. "When you said you were thinking about it, did you mean that you were thinking you want to do it?"

She looks at the row of charts that are hung along the wall in her office. "I've never done anything like it before. I'm not very adventurous. It might be fun."

"Seriously?" I ask without trying to contain any of the excitement I feel. "I'd love to draw you."

"Would I be able to stay anonymous? I don't want anyone to know it's me and I'm totally good with you selling it. Do I need to sign something?"

I nod. Since my drawings have started selling, Zoe took it upon herself to draw up a standard release form for me to have on hand for whenever I spotted someone I wanted to capture with my pencil. I've never worried before about any problems with the subjects of my drawings taking issue with the fact that they haven't granted me express permission, but now, that my work is gaining a larger audience, it's a prudent step to take.

"If you're really interested, I'll email you a copy of the form to sign and I can draw your profile so no one will ever know it's you."

She chuckles in a way that suggests that she's trying to find the humor in something that is making her incredibly uncomfortable. "It's just that I have a crazy ex-boyfriend. He's tracked me down a few times, so I don't want to draw any attention to myself."

I can't sympathize since all my former beaus have gladly dropped out of sight the hour after we broke up. "I'm really glad you'll pose for me. I can't wait to get started."

"Bridget." Her hand grazes my knee just as I'm about to stand. "Will you hang it in the gallery?"

I want to say yes because I hear the anticipation in her voice. I assume it's because she wants to see it there, on display even if no one but the two of us will know it's her. "I have a few weeks left at the gallery, so I think we can get it done before that."

"I probably don't need to say this, but thank you."

There's no reason for her to thank me. She may not realize it yet, but she's giving me a gift by agreeing to let me draw her. It's the creative fuel I need to get myself back on track.

# FIFTEEN

"Harper?" he repeats her name for a third time. "She works out of what facility?"

"The one that helped me do this." I perch both my brows as I pull my left hand into a fist. "I couldn't do that a week ago."

"The woman is a genius." He laughs as he pulls my balled fist to his lips. "I knew you'd be a spitfire when it came to recovery, but you're blowing me away with how well you're doing."

I love hearing those words from him. Our relationship is settling into something that's both familiar and exciting at the same time. The moment Dane arrived at my apartment after his shift, I'd launched into a fast paced retelling of my entire day.

His face had brightened when I told him about my interview. I had promised my confidence to both Tex and Harper about their portraits so I had only mentioned that I had found some subjects to sketch even though I've already gotten emails back from both of them with the signed contracts attached. He'd told me immediately that he was proud of me for chasing after my dreams and that he'd do anything it took to help me.

"Next week I'm going to start doing some light weights." I pull my hand free from his. "I'll be back to myself in no time flat."

"You're back to yourself now." He exhales audibly. "I've been thinking about you all day."

I know it's the words of a man who wants to fuck. I heard it wrapped within the growl of his tone when he called me earlier asking what time I'd be home. I felt it in the soft brush of his kiss on my cheek when he first got to my apartment and I see it now in his eyes.

"You want me," I say it brazenly, not caring that it sounds like a mirrored reflection of everything I'm feeling for him.

"I always want you." His hands slide down my back towards my ass. "This is the only the second time I've seen you in a dress."

I wish he would have seen me earlier, when I was first dressed. It's evening now and the sweater I pulled on over the black shift dress has caused it to wrinkle. My hair has lost the curl it first had when I let it air dry after my shower this morning. I'm not even sure if my make-up is still on my face or if it slid off during my ambitious, ten block, walk home in the warm late afternoon sun.

"I look like hell." I hold onto the front of the button down blue dress shirt he's wearing.

"You look breathtaking." His lips glide over mine slowly and right before they slip off, he pulls my bottom lip between his teeth. "I can barely control myself."

I smile against his mouth. "You don't have to."

"Is that an invitation to take you to bed?"

"You don't need an invitation, Dane," I whisper the words as I graze my lips over the early evening stubble that has settled on his chin.

He doesn't say another word. He reaches down to unbutton his pants, he pushes them down until his glorious hard cock is free and he looks me straight in the eye before he cocks a winged brow.

I lick my lips, reach for his hand to help lower me to my knees and I race my tongue over the head of his cock before I slide it into my eager mouth.

***

"Don't move, Bridget." His breath is faint on the bare skin of my back.

We're in my bedroom now. I'd licked and sucked his thick root until he was close to his release. I'd felt his body tighten in anticipation and just as I looked up into his face to ready my tongue to take it all, he'd yanked me to my feet, pulled my dress off and fallen to his knees to lick me.

I was so close from the heady taste of his flesh and the sounds he had been making when I was sucking him, that I came on his lips almost immediately.

He didn't waste but a minute before he scooped me into his arms, walked down the hallway while kissing me and then put me on my bed.

I'd said his name quietly as I watched him put on a condom. I'd smiled into his kiss when he adjusted my hips on the edge of the bed, and I'd covered my mouth with my hand as he pushed himself into me in one quick, jarring movement.

He'd taken me with a ferocity I've never felt before and after I climaxed, he'd slowed just enough to tease me with his fingers on my clit to bring me to the edge again. I felt the heated intensity bowl through me, but then he'd flipped me over onto my stomach and entered me from behind.

"I'm going to come," he purrs from behind me.

"Yes," I say in a tone that's so low that I doubt he can hear me.

He pushes into me with a fierce grunt. "I love fucking you. Your pussy is so tight."

I close my eyes to soak in the sensations. My body aches from the size of his cock. He's long, and in this position, it takes me to a place where the pain of its depth is mixed with the pleasure of his girth. It's almost too much and with each thrust, I whimper softly into the tangled sheets of my bed.

I feel his hands on my ass, as he rocks his body into mine. "I'm going to come so hard. Christ, it's going to be so good."

I still when I feel his hands tighten on the flesh of my hips and I listen as he calls out my name before he pumps himself into me, finally releasing everything he has.

# SIXTEEN

"Your cupboards are almost as empty as your refrigerator," he jokes as he walks back into my bedroom holding a tall glass of water. "You only have one glass left."

I reach forward to grab the water and I swallow half in one big gulp. "I was so thirsty. You wore me out."

"I wore you out?" His hand falls to his groin and he strokes his hand over his semi-hard cock. "You're the one who wears me out, Bridget."

"I like having sex with you," I confess because after what we just did, it's no secret that I take pleasure in everything he does to me intimately.

He takes back the glass and finishes the water before he brushes his hand over his lips. "I can't stand those sounds you make. Jesus. Those sounds are everything."

I blush. I've never been able to curb what I'm feeling during sex but with Dane the sounds that come from the depths of me as I'm crashing into an orgasm are guttural and loud. They're also unfamiliar. I can't contain them and tonight when he fucked me while I was on my stomach, I didn't even try to temper any of it. I just let my body express what it was feeling.

"I hope your new neighbors aren't going to mind."

"What?" I laugh as I pop up my brow. "What do you mean?"

"The walls in this place are paper thin." He nods towards one of the faded white walls of my bedroom. "Whoever lives next to you gets to hear everything we do."

"They do not." I cover my face with my hands, suddenly feeling self-conscious. "The woman who lives next to me is in her seventies."

"Damn." He places the glass on the nightstand before he yanks both of my feet from below the covers. "I hope she has her hearing aid turned off because I'm about to make you scream."

I don't struggle against the strength of his hands at all. I look up as he rests himself next to me and I let him part my legs before he glides his skilled fingers back over my wet folds.

***

"When are you moving?" He's on his feet, fully dressed and it's just past midnight.

I should ask him why he's not staying but I'm grateful that he's leaving. It's not because I don't take comfort in the warmth of his body when he's next to me while I sleep, but this is one of the last nights I'll have in this place and I need some time alone. "I get my new keys the day after tomorrow."

"It's fully furnished too?"

I nod. The furniture in my new place in Murray Hill is only slightly better than here, but it is a definite step up. I know I can afford something nicer but I'm not going to waste my savings on an apartment that I don't need. If it's safe, and affordable, I'm more than happy to call it home. It's also closer to Easton Pub so when I start back at work there next week, I'll have a much shorter subway ride home after my shifts.

"I took some pictures of it." I gesture towards the night stand. "They're on my phone."

He scoops it up and into his palm. I watch as his fingers skim across the screen. "I like this place already. It's bigger than this apartment."

It is. It also has an extra room just in case I decide to take on a roommate at some point. For now, I'm going to use the guestroom to store my drawings. I'm determined to take my art more seriously and to build on the interest that's already out there.

"Do you like the kitchen?" I lean forward to catch a glimpse of my phone's screen. "I can actually move around in that one."

He steps back so the phone is out of my view. I feel an instant pit in my stomach.

"Give me the phone, Dane, and I'll show you where I'm going to set up some easels for the drawings I'm working on."

He fumbles with the edge of the case and I know without any question that his eyes saw more than just the pictures of my new place. Even in the very dim light that is coming into the room from the hallway, I can see his hands are shaking.

"I should go." He hands the phone to me with a heavy shove. "I need to go."

I skim my thumb over the screen and open the photo app. I scan through the pictures seeing only those of my apartment and a few random people I'd captured with my camera with the hope that I'd find inspiration to draw them at some point. "What is it?"

"I'm working an early shift." He fidgets on his feet. "I'm going to crash at the station tonight."

"No," I say too loudly. "What did you see on my phone?"

He shoves a hand through his hair. "It's nothing. I'm tired. I'm going to take off."

Secrets have a way of revealing themselves even with the best efforts to keep them hidden. I'm not letting him walk out of here until I know what rattled him. "Did I take a picture of someone you know?"

His eyes dart down to my phone. "You took a picture of me when I was sleeping."

I had. I had done it one night after we'd made love and he had fallen asleep on his back with his arm over his head. He'd looked like something out of a magazine and I had stood on the bed above him, with a sheet wrapped around my body as I took one single picture of his chest and his face.

"Is that not okay?" I cradle the phone in my hands. "Do you want me to delete it? I really like it."

He takes one step closer to the bed. "Do you ever look at it?"

I lick my bottom lip knowing that there's absolutely no reason why I shouldn't be completely honest. "I look at it every day."

I watch as he struggles with what to say next. I see his eyes dart from my face to the phone. "I look so peaceful in that picture. I looked like that in the drawing you did of me too."

"That's how you look." I nod slightly. "You look like that."

"No." He stares at me, his eyes locked on mine. "You see me differently than anyone ever has before."

I swear I feel something shift between us with those words. He has to feel it too because he pulls me to my feet, wraps his arms around my nude body and kisses me before he tucks me into bed and leaves without another word.

# SEVENTEEN

"Have you seen Vanessa lately?" Zoe picks up another cardboard box before she places it right back in the same spot.

"No." I try to contain a giggle at her misplaced desire to help me move. Two of the cooks from the pub had offered a hand, and a car. I was grateful and because of my sparse wardrobe and the few items I'd accumulated since I moved into my old place, it had only taken two trips to get everything I own in the world into the foyer of my new place.

She kicks the edge of the box with her sneaker before she lowers herself into a tan colored rocking chair. "Where does this box go?"

I can sense that she's looking for a one way ticket back to her Park Avenue apartment so I hand it right to her. "I'm not going to unpack everything today. I'll take care of it tomorrow."

She doesn't even try to hide the wide smile that takes over her mouth. "Are you sure?"

The only thing I'm sure of is that Zoe may have the best intentions, but the actual moving part isn't her strong suit. "It's all good. You were a big help today."

I mean it. She'd embraced me as we said goodbye to my old place and she'd toasted with a bottle of water to the good times we'd shared there. I felt absolutely nothing but hope as I closed the door for the last time.

"You didn't answer my question." She crosses her legs at the ankles as I struggle to open a box marked for the kitchen.

"About Vanessa? She was doing some seminar thing." I pull a coffee mug wrapped in tissue paper from the box. "It was a training thing. I think she said she'd be done next week."

"I think I remember that now." She gestures towards the kitchen. "You should wash out all the cupboards before you put your dishes away."

"Why?" I yank another mug out of the overstuffed box.

"My mother told me that before I moved to Manhattan." She shrugs her shoulders.

I laugh at her passed-on motherly advice. "Speaking of mothers, mine wants to come to check out my new place."

My mother had called me early this morning, waking me before dawn. She's always been a morning person and even though my father and I preferred to sleep in, that never deterred her from arranging family hikes and getaway trips that always had to start before most people even thought about leaving the comfort of their beds.

"Your mom is great," she begins before she laughs softly. "The night of your accident, she kept talking about how she hopes you'll get married soon so she can have a grandchild."

"Can't you just loan me Vane for when she comes over?" I cock a brow. "She could play with him and it would give me some breathing room."

"He's all yours whenever you want him." She sweeps her hands in the air in front of her. "Your mom was great with him. She was also a mess when she heard you got hit by a car."

I know that. I saw it in her face when they'd let her into the ER room they'd taken me into. She had sobbed uncontrollably while she'd clung to my father. I'll never forget that moment and it's one of the few reasons why I want her to come visit me. I know that she needs to see me more often.

"It was really hard for her." I turn back towards the box. "It would have been too much for her if I…"

"Don't say it." I hear a rustle behind me before her arms circle my shoulders. "It would have been too much for all of us. You scared the shit out of me, Bridge. It devastated Vanessa. We need you so much."

I clasp both my hands over hers. "When she's done with the seminar, you'll both come over for dinner, okay?"

"It's a date. I'll go now so you can get back to work."

I laugh as I turn to embrace her. This is the start of my new beginning and there's one person I can't wait to see.

# EIGHTEEN

"I feel like I haven't seen you in a week." I wrinkle my nose realizing how pathetic that sounds. It's only been four days since he left my apartment after seeing his picture on my phone.

He flicks open the napkin in front of him and places it across his lap before he scoops one of the warm pieces of bread from the basket the waiter just dropped off. "I had to cover someone's shift. I didn't have to but I owed him one."

I could tell by the weariness in his voice last night when he called me to say goodnight that he was exhausted. I know that he loves his job but I see the toll the physical demands take on him. He's sitting in front of me now, in a crowded bistro, less than a block from my new apartment, with a growth of beard on his face, and a tired look in his eyes.

"You're a good guy."

"I'm a good guy?" he repeats back with a wide grin. "I'm not a great lover? I'm not the sexiest man you've ever known?"

I try to hide the small smile that is tugging at the edge of my lips by taking a bite of the bread.

"That's the game you're going to play with me?" He lifts the bread in his hand in the air before tipping his chin towards me. "I actually like that you think I'm a good guy."

I cover my mouth with my hand while I chew and swallow. "I bet everyone who knows you thinks you're a good guy."

The playfulness that is there in his eyes disappears with the next blink he takes. He bites into the bread again as his gaze floats over the interior of the bistro. I know immediately where his mind has darted off to, so I pull it back in.

"I'm going to start on two new portraits tomorrow."

When he looks at me again I see a calm softness in the lines of his brow. "Who are they of?"

"Both of them are women," I begin before I lean back to let the waiter place a small garden salad in front of me. I wait until he gives Dane his before I continue. "One is the wife of a man I met a week ago and the other is a really beautiful woman I know."

"She can't possibly be more beautiful than you." He stabs his fork into a piece of tomato before scooping it into his mouth.

My mouth curves. "She's gorgeous. She has dark hair, bright green eyes. She should have been a model."

He licks a wayward drop of salad dressing from his bottom lip. "What does she do?"

I know that I promised Harper I wouldn't tell anyone about her portrait, but this is Dane and there's no harm in sharing some masked details with him. "I met her when I went for physical therapy."

"It's your therapist?" He munches on a leaf of lettuce. "Her name is Harper, right?"

The only way out of this is to avoid the direct questions completely so I do. "The other woman is older. I mean she's older than we are. She's been married to the same man for thirty years."

"What's she like?"

I've only spoken to Tex's wife, Leanna, once on the phone but the energy that flowed through her voice is witness to the fact that she's a bundle of positivity. "I haven't met her in person yet, but I talked to her on the phone. I think she'll be fun to work with."

We eat in silence, both watching the other. When he finally pushes his plate aside, he clears his throat. "I'm really proud of you, Bridget. You're the most remarkable person I've ever known."

They aren't words you expect to hear when you have a forkful of food in your mouth. I cough slightly, hoping that the piece of lettuce that just slid down my throat whole won't choke me. I chew quickly, wanting to say something about how touching his words are but the moment is lost when the waiter returns with our entrees.

Dane blows out a puff of air between his lips as soon as we're alone again. "You're really important to me. You're becoming really important to me."

I fumble with my hands, knowing that they're simply a physical reflection of what I'm feeling inside. I want to abandon the dinner and go back to my apartment. I want to crawl into his lap and kiss him until I can't tell if the breath I taste is mine or his. I want to say things that are there inside of my heart, but my mind is keeping them under lock and key.

"I know you hate the Maisy stuff." He hangs his head down. "I hate the fucking Maisy stuff."

I can't make the emotional leap from hearing him tell me that I'm important to talking about the woman he was about to propose to when we met. "Don't talk about her."

"I know it tears you up inside." He shakes his shoulders. "I don't know exactly what you feel but I see the pain in your face when I bring her up."

I reach for my napkin so I can cover my quivering hands in my lap. "I just want that part of your life to be over."

"I need it to be done." He rakes his hand through his hair. "I'm going to take care of it this week. If I have to give her the house, I will."

I can't respond. There's nothing I can say that will offer anything that even remotely conveys what I'm feeling inside.

"I want to build a future with you, Bridget. I want that more than anything."

I move my lips to tell him that I want it too but he's still talking.

"I won't rush you into anything, but I've never felt the way I do when I'm with you. I'll do whatever it takes to show you that my past is in my past."

I look down at my untouched dinner. "Can you take me home? I just want to go home."

He doesn't hesitate before he's on his feet. He rifles through his wallet, throws some bills on the table and takes me by the hand.

# NINETEEN

We roll over the mattress entangled in each other's clothing. I'd tried to pull off my clothes but he'd had me on the bed before I had a chance to undo the zipper on my jeans. Now, his hands are desperately clawing at the t-shirt I'm wearing while I work to pull the bulky sweater he has on, over his head.

He finally stills for a moment. "Let me undress you. I want to see you."

I should point out that it's hard to distinguish anything in my bedroom. The window coverings in my new place do the job they're intended to do. I can't see any of the light from the surrounding buildings or the street. It's dark and when I fell asleep last night, I'd relished in the calm that came with the darkness and also the muted street noise.

I pull on his hands but he slides quickly off the bed to turn on the small light on the nightstand. It may have been designed for reading but anyone who hoped to do that, would struggle to make out the words. It's dim and right now, it's throwing off a romantic tone that is perfect.

I lay still as he slowly removes each article of my clothing. He stops when the only thing I have on is a pair of panties. His hands trace a path over my stomach and hip bones before they come to rest on the sides of the black lace. "I tell you all the time that you're beautiful."

I reach up to grab hold of his broad shoulders. I want to kiss him. I need to feel my mouth on his. "Kiss me."

He leans down without any hesitation and kisses me deeply, his tongue licking its way into my mouth. "I love kissing you, Bridget."

I pull him close, wanting to taste his lips again. I moan into the depth of his kiss. I weave my fingers through his hair and he groans softly into my mouth.

He lowers himself onto me, his jean covered groin rubbing tenderly against my flesh. My hand darts down to the waistband. I crave the touch of his hard flesh. I ache to feel him inside of me.

In an instant he circles my waist with his hand and flips us over so I'm on top of him. I straddle his broad thighs, pushing myself up so my body is on display.

His eyes scan my face before they drop to my breasts. They're not large and at one time I may have wished they were more generous but now, seeing the desire in his eyes, I know that they're enough. I know instinctively that I'm enough for him.

"You don't know what you do to me." His hand leaps to his bare chest. "I feel like I can't breathe when you look at me."

I push my chin down. I don't want my eyes to betray me. I know that he can see things when he looks at me. I know it's not just about the desperate pull that my body feels for his. It's not just about the fact that I can't hide a smile when I catch him looking at me. It's about the way my heart feels when I hear him say my name. It's about the fact that he told me, not more than an hour ago, that he'd give up the house that he saved his entire life for, if it means we can move forward in peace together.

"I tell myself to slow down." He slides his hands over my thighs. "I keep telling myself that I'm going to scare you away, but I can't help it."

"We'll take it slowly," I say softly as I lean forward to brush my lips over his cheek. "We'll take it one day at a time."

His hands circle my waist, as he pulls my body into his chest. "I've wasted most of my life not knowing you. I can't waste another minute."

I give in to his kiss and his hands as he grabs hold of the thin lace of my panties and rips them from me.

***

I feel the weight of his body when he returns to the bed. After we'd kissed and he'd licked me until I begged him to stop, he'd held me in his strong arms. He'd talked softly about wanting to watch me sketch portraits, and a dream he'd had last week about us hiking a mountain trail together.

He'd gone to the kitchen to get us each a glass of juice and when he returned, he'd finally pushed his jeans and boxer briefs down. I had turned over then to catch my breath but I heard the faint sound of my nightstand drawer opening and the unmistakable tear of the foil of the condom package.

His breathing had shifted and I knew without looking that he was sheathing his hard cock so he could finally take me the way I'd wanted him to all night. I'd pleaded with him to fuck me when I came the first time under his tongue, but he had ignored me and instead, slid one of his long fingers into my channel until he found the tender spot that pushed me back over the edge in an instant.

"Bridget." His lips are on my neck. "Turn over for me."

I do and just as I'm about to pull in a heavy breath, his hands are on my thighs, pushing them apart as he settles between them. He pushes my hands to the side as his mouth dives down to claim my right nipple. I moan loudly from the sensation of his teeth grazing over the swollen bud. He sucks on it harder, pulling a thread of desire from deep within my body. I try to move my legs to quiet the desperate need that I feel in my core.

"My body aches for you." His words are muffled by own flesh. "I'm so hard."

I try to twist my arm so that I can reach down to circle my hand around his thick root but he shakes his head.

I whimper, not as much out of frustration for the denial but more for the yearning that I feel inside. I want him to make love to me. I want him to slide his cock into me while he kisses me. I want him to take me slowly tonight, but at this point, it's not about my need, it's about his desire to own my body and when he pulls back from my breast to look into my face, I know that he won't temper what he's feeling. He's going to drive himself into me until I scream his name as I claw his back.

Not a word is spoken between us as he rallies back on his heels and thrusts his cock into me.

The connection takes my breath away because it's different tonight. It's not just about his need to get off. It has nothing to do with me chasing an orgasm. It's about two people who are baring themselves in every possible way for the other.

His hips grind into me as a string of muted curse words fall from his lips. His eyes never leave mine and as I feel my body tense with intense pleasure, he mouths three words that I'm not ready to hear yet. I close my eyes as I race over the edge knowing that nothing between us will ever be the same again.

# TWENTY

"I think we're done, Bridget."

I turn to look at where she's standing near the desk in her office. It's my last scheduled therapy visit with Harper and I hate to admit it, but I'm going to miss the encouragement she's been quick to offer me. "I'm good to go?"

"You shouldn't overdo it." She nods towards my left hand. "The bone is healed but it's going to be weak for a few months. Take it slow and steady and you'll be set."

It's the words that I've been longing to hear. The accident was more than two months ago now, but it feels like a lifetime ago. So much has changed and later today, when I go see Ben, for my check-up, I already know that I'll receive just as promising news from him too. I've been diligent about following every suggestion the medical professionals have offered me.

"You're doing a follow-up with Dr. Foster after lunch?"

I smile. "You can read minds. I was just thinking about that."

She raises both brows. "I can't read minds. I wish I could."

It's an open invitation to ask what that means but for now, we're still just therapist and patient. She's cancelled our portrait sessions twice and I know that her weak excuse about having to catch up on paperwork was nothing more than a diversion because she's having second thoughts about putting herself out there. Regardless of how much I've assured her that I won't draw her in a way that makes her recognizable, she's wary and I can't blame her for that.

"Do you still want to draw me?"

I try to hide the fact that I'm completely taken aback by the question. "I'd love to draw you."

"I don't have another appointment until four. Can we start now?"

I jump off of the exam table, reach into my bag and pull out my sketchpad and pencil. "Now is the perfect time to start."

***

"Are you in relationship, Bridget?" She doesn't turn her head away from the point on the wall that I asked her to focus on thirty minutes ago. She'd sat in complete silence while I outlined the curves of her brow and chin.

I don't see any reason not to be forthcoming so I put it all out there. "I am. We met a few months ago."

"What's he like?"

I've never actually described Dane to anyone. Zoe met him, so there's been no need to explain to her that I see him as this once-in-a-lifetime kind of guy. Vanessa may not know him well but she sees him through the eyes of soon-to-be family member. She'll marry Garrett and Dane will become her cousin-in-law. I have no idea how close their extended family is but judging by what Dane told me about his mother and Garrett's mom, Vanessa will be a part of Dane's life forever.

I push my hair back behind my ear before I start shading in her hairline. "He's kind, he's compassionate. He has a really good heart."

"Are you in love with him?"

These aren't the questions I imagined I'd have to answer when I came into her office more than an hour ago. I also didn't think I'd be drawing her profile.

"I like him a lot," I say honestly. "I can see myself falling in love with him in time. I don't want to rush into anything."

"You're too young to be that wise," she mutters through a half grin. "I rushed into my last relationship and it didn't end well."

"You talked about that before," I offer hoping it helps her to open up more. We're not friends. If anything we're barely acquaintances, but she needs to unload, and if I'm the person she sees fit to do that with, I'm more than willing to sit and listen. "You said he tracked you down. Is that the same guy?"

"That's him." She turns towards me briefly before she settles her gaze back on the wall. "I don't know how he found me, but he did. He was here yesterday."

I can't imagine that. I've never had a man chase me beyond a few boys on the playground when I was a child. "I'm sorry to hear that. Is he dangerous?"

"Not in that way." She rubs her hand over her eyes. "Emotionally he's dangerous. He hurt me. He dumped me and then begged me to take him back."

My mind jumps to Maisy and although I know that Dane never begged her to take him back, the pain of the rejection has stung her enough that she's had trouble letting him go. "That sounds awful."

"I've never loved anyone but him and yesterday when he was here he told me he loves me too and wants to try again."

It sounds so cut and dry but I know that if it was, she wouldn't be confiding in me. "What do you want?"

"I want to understand him. I want to know if he's playing games with me."

I nod because I can't think of anything to say that will help her.

She drops her chin slightly, which changes the shape of her eye. I quickly sketch its outline wanting to capture the pure emotion that I see there. "If I give him one more chance, and he breaks my heart again, I don't know if I can survive that."

The pencil in my hand stops in mid-air. I look up and that's when I see a solitary tear running down her beautiful face.

# TWENTY-ONE

The moment to capture her portrait had been lost when she'd started to cry. I'd reached forward not sure if offering her the comfort of an embrace would help her. She hadn't even glanced in my direction before she pulled a tissue from a box on her desk, and wiped the tear away as if it, or the emotion behind it, never existed.

She'd closed herself up then and as I gathered together my things, she promised that she'd call me to finish the portrait. I know that she won't. The moment of vulnerability that took her to a place where she felt she could open up, had disappeared. I'll work with what I have on paper and the memory of her face in my mind's eye and I'll finish the sketch.

I feel the vibration of my phone in my pocket as I walk out of the lobby of Harper's building and into the languid heat of the late morning. I scoop the phone out, feeling a sharp burst of pain in my wrist when I do.

I glance down at the screen, realizing that the sunlight's reflection is making it impossible for me to read the text message. I push my bag onto my shoulder as I cup my hand over the phone's screen to block out the light.

It's a text message from Zoe.

**Vanessa can have dinner tomorrow. Your place at six?**

I type out a quick text back to her.

**Works for me. You bring the white wine.**

I smile knowing that the message will bring a smile to her face.

I take a step forward before my breath catches in my throat when I feel a large hand circle my waist. I've never been mugged and in my imagination when it did happen, it wouldn't be on a busy street in the middle of the day. I always thought it would happen when I left a club at night alone.

I ready myself to scream when I hear his voice in my ear. "How did you end up in the very spot in Manhattan that I am?"

I pivot on my heel, looking up into his dark eyes. "It's fate."

"Call it whatever you want, Bridget." Dane lowers his face until his lips are level with mine. "I call it destiny."

***

"You didn't follow me to my appointment, did you?" I rest my hand on his thigh. "I know I didn't tell you that I had a therapy appointment today, so the only way you would have known that is if you were following me."

"You're a creature of habit." He scoops my hand into his palm before he brings it to his lips for a kiss. "You kept all of your accident paperwork on the kitchen table in your old apartment, and you do the same in your new place."

He's right. I did dump everything into my purse before I left the old place and I dumped it all onto the table at the apartment in Murray Hill the minute I arrived there. It may not be the best filing system, but it's working for me. "You looked through those papers?"

"Those papers are a mess, Bridget. You write notes on napkins, and paper bags and take-out menus."

"I do that." I nod.

"I sat at the table to drink the coffee I made myself the other morning when you were still asleep." He grazes his hand over the back of my hair. "I was reading a magazine you had there about some beauty products."

I pull my hand up to stifle a giggle. "You didn't read that, did you?"

"I bought some stuff so I can exfoliate tonight."

I shake my head, not certain whether he's joking or not. "Your skin is perfect the way it is."

"Spoken by a true beauty expert." He nuzzles his chin into the side of my hair. "You wrote the details about your appointment today on the cover of that magazine. It was scribbled across the face of the model."

I remember doing that when Harper's office manager had called to tell me that she needed to change my appointment so it was a day earlier than scheduled. "It was the closest thing I had to write on."

"I saw it as a sign from the heavens above that I was supposed to meet you there so I could buy you a coffee."

I look down at my empty hands. "You forgot the coffee part."

"I can do one better." He points to where a hotdog vendor is standing at the entrance to Central Park. "I can go over there and get my favorite girl a hotdog for lunch, with a pretzel for dessert."

"I'm your favorite girl?"

"You're the only girl in the world."

I stumble over my emotions as I nod faintly knowing that they're not just words meant to romance me, they're coming from his heart and they're pulling every one of my emotions right to the surface.

# TWENTY-TWO

"I'm sorry I can't stay for your appointment, but I'm working tonight. I need to work every night this week."

I look up into his face as we stand in the lobby of the hospital. I need to check-in for my appointment with Ben in five minutes. I know he's likely running late but I don't want to hold him up. "I need to get up there."

"Do you have plans tonight? Can I call you on my break?"

"You can call me anytime you want." I glance over his shoulder at the large clock hanging on the wall. "Did you want to talk about something in particular?"

"I hate to do this now when you have to go."

The words stall me. I know what he's about to say. It's Maisy. We've been blissfully avoiding the subject of his ex-girlfriend since he told me he was willing to give up his house for her. I didn't take that statement literally. I had hoped that we could talk about it more and that I could reassure him that I wanted to be a sounding board for him if he needed that. He has a right to at least the portion of the investment he made in that property and now that I know that he'd sacrifice so much for me, I want to help him get back what's rightfully his.

"Is it about Maisy?" I ask with little noticeable emotion in my voice. I want to be mature about this. I want him to understand that I don't feel threatened by her, even if I did at one time.

"I think I have a solution for all of that." He pulls me into his arms. "I think I found a way to finally get her out of my life."

"And out of the house?" I ask.

"I know you have to go but I've realized that I don't want to live there anymore. I can't live there. I was there with her."

I rest my head against his hard chest. "Will you just sell it?"

"If I moved back in, I'd see her in every room and I'd never be able to bring you there. That was the house I shared with her. I want to start fresh and new."

The idea of him selling the property and then giving Maisy something to compensate her for her contributions to their living expenses seems more than fair to me. "Have you talked to her about this?"

He pulls back suddenly. "You have a minute to get up there. You need to go. Tell Ben it's my fault if he asks you why you're late."

I look into his eyes. "You'll come see me tomorrow after you sleep, right?"

"I'll be there as soon as I can."

***

"I was going to suggest we take another x-ray of your wrist, but I don't think that's necessary." Ben squeezes his fingers near my thumb. "This doesn't hurt, does it?"

"No." I watch as he bends each of my fingers.

"Have you experienced any pain at all?"

"I hurt it earlier when I was reaching into my pocket to pull out my phone."

He nods. "You're going to get that from time-to-time. If it happens often, come back in and I'll take a look at it."

I look past him to a poster hanging on the wall of the human skeletal system. "Are my ribs fully healed?"

"Ribs are tricky." He moves his gloved hand to my side. "Lift your arms over your head."

I do. "What do you mean tricky?"

He doesn't say a word as he runs his fingers over my side. "You're the best judge of how they're healing. If the pain has subsided, you're on the right track."

"I don't feel any pain in my side." I drop my hands when he turns towards a tablet that is resting on the edge of the exam table.

"Any headaches?"

It's a question no one has asked me for weeks. I expected to have splitting headaches after my head crashed into the windshield of the police car, but that hadn't happened. The pain radiating from my forehead had been intense for a few days and then it had disappeared. I'd gone home with a stern warning about reporting any unusual symptoms including loss of memory or balance, but I had been fine. The worse thing had been a slight ringing in my ears, which my mother had reported to the nurse on call in the ER. She assured us it was normal and that with rest it would pass.

"My head is fine."

"Have you thought about being a stunt woman?"

I giggle at the suggestion. It's the same thing he said to me the day I was discharged. "You've already used that joke on me."

"I know." He darts his head to the side so our eyes meet. "I was testing your memory."

I slide off the edge of the exam table and onto my feet. "I can go now, right? There must be other people waiting to see you who are actually sick."

He cocks a brow when I brush past him on my way to the door. "Take care of yourself, Bridget and take care of Dane too. He's one of the good ones."

I smile knowing that he already knows I see and feel that. I don't need anyone to remind me that the man I can't stop thinking about is almost too good to be true.

# TWENTY-THREE

"I thought you said that your boyfriend was going to be here."

I had said that. Call it wishful thinking but yesterday when Dane told me that he'd be here after he woke up, I decided that asking Zoe to come over early would give them an opportunity to get to know each other better. I'm not one of those women who need the absolute approval of her friends in order to fall in love with a man, but I want to know that my closest friend sees what I see in Dane.

In some ways I regret telling Zoe about Maisy and Dane's almost engagement and I wish I hadn't confided in her about the struggle he was facing over his house, but she knows those things now and if I can counter those first impressions with a few minutes of one-on-one time between the two of them, I want to do that.

When I'd called him earlier to ask what time he'd be stopping by, he'd told me that he had a few errands to run before his shift tonight and he couldn't make it. My heart had sunk, not just because I wouldn't get the chance to see him but because it meant I'd have to explain to Zoe why he wasn't here when she got here.

"He had stuff to do," I say with a heavy sigh. "I'm going to start back at the pub at the end of the week so I don't know when I'll get a chance to get you two together again."

"You'll invite him to the pub when he has a night off." She wraps her arm around my shoulder. "I'll stop by to have a glass of white wine and I'll visit with him."

I tap my hand over hers. "You'd do that?"

"You have no idea how much your face lights up when you talk about him." She squeezes her side into mine. "I've never seen you act like that about a guy."

"I've never known anyone like him, Zoe."

"I said that to you when I met Beck." She laughs. "Or I thought it. He was different. I knew there was something special about him."

"I know that about Dane too."

"We've got a couple of hours before Vanessa gets here so what do you want to do?"

I point at the last few boxes that I stacked in the corner of my living room. "I need to unpack those. You game for that?"

"I'm game." She reaches for the half full glass of white wine she poured for herself when she arrived. "Let me finish this and I'll help."

I laugh as I brush past her to pick up the first box.

***

"I like this so much better than your last apartment." Vanessa pushes past me to look down the hallway. "I'm sorry I was late, Bridge. There was way too much going on at the hospital today."

I don't ask. Every time I've ever asked about her work, she launches into a rant that's filled with medical terms that make no sense at all to me. I admire her for having the drive to chase after her dream of being a nurse. I just don't understand any of the medical jargon or how she can stay so cheery when she's facing so much illness on a daily basis.

"I was early. I came to meet her boyfriend but he never showed," Zoe spits the words out.

She's had more than a few glasses of wine. I'd peg it at three but while I was busy unloading the last of the boxes containing my belongings, she was playing a game on my tablet and downing the wine like it was water.

Thankfully Vanessa is so busy texting someone on her smartphone that she doesn't hear a word that Zoe just said.

"You should see her studio." Zoe pulls on Vanessa's elbow. "She has some of her drawings set up in there."

Vanessa's eyes darts up. "You have a studio here?"

"No." I half-shrug my shoulder. "It's not an actual studio. It's a spare bedroom."

"Show me." Vanessa's gaze moves towards the hallway. "There's a three alarm fire, I may need to go back into work depending on the number of injured. We're short staffed right now."

I glance down at her phone. It's too early for Dane to be at work yet which offers a strange sense of comfort I didn't think I'd need. I saw him in his gear the night of my accident. I know that he's trained to protect not only himself, but the people he works alongside, during a fire. I'm just grateful when I know that he's safe.

"I'll turn it on." I brush past her and Zoe. "You two go look at my spare room. I'll be right there."

I hear them walking the tiled floor toward the far end of the hallway as I push the button on my remote to turn on the television. I don't watch it often but when I do it's almost always tuned onto the news channel so I'm not surprised when a reporter sitting behind an anchor desk pops onto the screen. She's talking about a shark attack in a remote area of the world and just as I turn toward the hallway I hear my name being called.

"Bridget, get in here now."

"I'm coming," I call back to Zoe as I steal one last glance at the television.

The image that greets me is completely different now. It's a male reporter. He's standing outside the smoldering shell of a house in Queens. I stare, open mouthed at the rushed scene of the fireman milling about, all working hard to save the neighboring homes. It's utter chaos and the chilling site of a woman on her knees crying as the camera pans over her quickly, stops my breath.

This is Dane's life. This is what he faces each and every time he goes to work. I want to call him. I want to tell him that I'm falling in love with him so that tonight, when he gets called to an emergency, he'll have those words in his heart.

"Bridget." Zoe's voice is more demanding.

I drop the remote onto the coffee table as I turn on my heel to rush down the hallway.

# TWENTY-FOUR

"You can't possibly be right." Zoe is looking directly at Vanessa when I enter the room. "You're wrong."

"I'm telling you I'm right." Vanessa is standing with her hands on her hips. "I've met her. That's her."

"Who did you meet?" I step between them, wanting to lessen the tension in the room. "What are you two talking about?"

"You drew Maisy," Vanessa says the words as her eyes race over my face.

I reach out in front of me to steady my balance. "What are you talking about? I never drew Maisy."

"That's her, Bridget." Her fingers float past my head towards one of the sketches I have displayed on the easels. "I'd know her anywhere."

I can't focus on the portraits, only on her words. "When I first asked you about Dane, you told me you'd never met him. How would you know what Maisy looks like?"

"Dane's mom introduced us a few weeks ago." She takes a step towards the portraits. "They were at the hospital for an appointment. I actually saw them there together yesterday but I was too busy to stop and talk. Dane was there too."

I can't absorb anything she's saying to me. "I think you're wrong."

"I'm not wrong. That's her. You drew her."

I stare at her and it feels as if the world is moving in slow motion as she steps away from me towards the easel that is displaying the portrait of Harper.

I feel an immediate sense of relief.

"That's not Maisy." I point towards the drawing. "It's not her. That's my physical therapist. Her name is Harper."

"No. I'm not talking about that one. It's the one over there. "Vanessa's head turns slowly to the left before she gestures towards a lone easel that I'd set up next to the window.

It holds the portrait that's meant the most to me. It's one of the ones that Dane cradled in his hands when he first saw my work.

I remember the day I drew it.

I remember the vulnerability in the woman's face when she looked at me and realized what I was doing.

It was then that she motioned for me to join her.

I did and as I stood next to her in the museum that morning, she told me about how she loved a man who accepted her exactly as she was. They were going to be married soon and live the life she'd always wanted. He was meeting her there, within the hour, to choose a new piece of artwork for their house from the gift shop. She wanted a print of a painting they'd both fallen in love with.

I'd stared at her face, soaking in the obvious joy she was feeling.

I'd hugged her tightly before I told her that I'd keep her in my good thoughts.

I scan the portrait of her hair cascading around her shoulders and her listless legs tucked under the blanket as she sat in the wheelchair she'd been in since she could remember.

As we said goodbye, she told me that she'd never felt the ground beneath her feet. She clasped my hands in hers and whispered in a shaky voice that on her honeymoon, the man she loved was going to carry her to the sand so she could see it between her toes. I'd smiled at the simplicity of that, knowing that it would be a gift that she'd keep inside of her forever.

Before I'd left the museum that day, I'd seen her again near the gift shop.

My breath catches in my chest as I remember the dark haired man who had crouched with his back to me in front of her. He'd pulled the blanket down slightly to reveal the curve of her stomach under the patterned blouse she was wearing and as he'd bent forward to kiss the top of her very swollen belly, she'd rested her chin against his hair.

"We're having a baby boy," she had called across the crowded room towards me before I waved with a smile and walked away.

"When did you draw that?" Zoe's hand is on my shoulder. I know it's meant to offer comfort but I feel nothing at all.

I swallow hard.

I turn towards her and reach for her hand for support. I feel my bottom lip quiver so I pull in a deep breath. "I drew it the day before I met Dane."

# EMBER

## PART THREE

NEW YORK TIMES &
USA TODAY BESTSELLING AUTHOR
DEBORAH BLADON

# ONE

"He left her?" Zoe can't contain the obvious confused agitation in her voice. "Is she in a wheelchair, Bridget?"

I glance back at the portrait. When I had walked up to the woman in the museum that day, I had shown her the drawing. Her hand had swept over the paper and she'd asked where the wheelchair was. I was silent, not because it made me uncomfortable, but because I had no understanding of whether the omission of it bothered her or not.

She must have sensed my trepidation because she quietly insisted that I include it, in an abstract way. I had. I had drawn the curves of the wheels and the straight and solid lines of the arms and back of the chair so they were understated. It was apparent, but not the focal point of the drawing. I wanted her spirit to rise above any other part of the portrait and when I showed her what I had done, she had smiled brilliantly. She'd whispered that she felt beautiful. I had told her she was.

"She was sitting in the cafeteria with Dane's mom when I met her," Vanessa interjects. "I was rushing back to my shift after a break so I didn't notice the wheelchair, but she was in it yesterday when I saw them down the hallway."

The confirmation only adds to the pain that has rushed through me. I'd had a conversation with Maisy. I'd listened to her talk about Dane and within those words I could sense the deep love she felt for him. They were having a son and each time that I've shared my body with him since that day, I've taken something from her whether I've known it or not. I've stolen her happiness. She doesn't deserve that.

I may not understand the intricacies of their relationship but I know what I saw. I saw a man lovingly kiss the pregnant belly of a woman. I saw tenderness and affection. How could he go from feeling all of that to leaving her a little more than a day later?

"Have you shown that to Dane?" Vanessa asks before her smartphone's ring pierces the air.

Zoe and I stand in silence as Vanessa mutters something into the stillness about an emergency, the hospital being short staffed and her need to rush back there.

"We should talk about this, Bridge." She pushes her phone back into the pocket of her sweater. "Why don't you ride over to the hospital with me in a taxi? We can talk on the way and then you can hop the subway back here."

"I should probably just go with you." Zoe waves her smartphone in the air. "Beck isn't home yet and the sitter needs to go. I'll share a taxi with you, Vanessa. Bridget can stay here."

She hasn't glanced at her phone since she arrived. I know she's made up an excuse because she can sense my need to be alone. She's always been able to gauge when the solace of my own company is the one thing I crave.

I don't move when Vanessa, and then Zoe, hugs me. Zoe's face darts into my line of sight for a brief moment. The confusion within her eyes is a pure reflection of my own feelings. I don't open my mouth to offer any explanation about how I unintentionally drew the woman Dane loved because I still can't get a firm grasp on the irony of it.

I don't ask Vanessa for any details about Maisy and her baby because it's not her story to tell. It's Dane's and the fact that we've shared our bodies and small pieces of our hearts with one another doesn't matter at this point. The only thing that truly matters is that the day before I met him, he was in the gift shop of a museum, picking out a print to hang on the wall of the home he shared with the woman he is going to have a baby with.

I stand in my makeshift studio as I hear the door of my apartment closing as my friends take leave to go share a ride where they'll talk about the man who helped nurse me back to health. They'll discuss the fact that I had no idea that I'd met Dane's ex-girlfriend. As they say goodbye when the taxi stops in front of the hospital to drop off Vanessa, they'll both take comfort in the fact that they are loved by men who don't carry secrets with the same weight of Dane's.

My hands tentatively reach for the portrait. The ache to hold it against my chest so I can weep for what might have been between Dane and me is only silenced by the almost uncontrollable drive I feel to destroy it.

It's haunting in that it captures a human spirit that is too brave and determined to give up. I'd seen the strength in Maisy's eyes when she'd called me over that day in the museum. She wasn't in search of pity or compassionate words. She wanted me to see her and not what had altered her life in such a significant way. Her smile and the light that radiated from within her were contagious and inspiring.

I'd left the museum that day with her words about love and promise ringing in my ears. I'd called Zoe to tell her that I wanted to meet Larry. I yearned for the promise of a future with a man who adored me. I wanted what Maisy had and because of a twist of fate, I have it now. I have Dane and she has a baby on the way.

I soak in the fine lines that my pencil had captured as I sat and watched Maisy. I hadn't bothered to ask her name, and she hadn't offered. It wasn't important then. It didn't matter the night that Dane sat on my bed, in my old apartment, while he studied the drawing. Until now, Maisy has been a faceless woman who was left behind in the restaurant. I may have felt a flash of compassion for her back then, but I'd gleefully grabbed hold of the man who decided his path didn't align with hers.

She's not just anyone now. She's the bright and beautiful woman I've had a brief conversation with. She's going to be a mom and for the rest of her son's life, he's going to look to Dane for guidance, acceptance and love.

I hear my smartphone ringing in the distance but the emotional energy it takes to answer it, isn't there. I don't want to hear Zoe ask if I'm going to be okay. I don’t want to compare notes with Vanessa about meeting Maisy.

As soon as the incessant ringing stops, it begins again and I close my eyes, willing it to quiet. I can't answer if it's Dane either. I can't bear the thought of hearing his voice. It will be filled with the carefree promise that it always is and I'll have to ask him questions that I don't want to hear the answers to.

I ignore the shrill bite of the smartphone's ring as I turn on my heel with Maisy's portrait lazily dangling between my fingers. I cross the hall to my own bedroom, place the drawing onto the foot of the bed and lower my head to my pillow. As I close my eyes, I know that when I open them again, nothing will ever be the same.

# TWO

"Dane didn't pick up when I tried to call him."

Zoe's head darts up. Her eyes scan my face for a brief second before they fall back down to Vane. I'd arrived on her doorstep, or more specifically, in the lobby of her building, shortly after sunrise.

Brighton had answered when I'd pushed the buzzer for the penthouse. He'd pulled me into his arms in a warm embrace when I walked over the threshold and into their home. The light from the day's break was just beginning to pour into the lavish space and I'd stood for a moment, feeling his strong arms around me, knowing that Zoe must have filled his ears, and mind, with words about the shock that had settled over me once I realized that I'd met Dane's ex-girlfriend.

"When did you try and call him?" She handily buttons the jumper she dressed Vane in after giving him a bath. "Was it last night or this morning?"

It was both. I'd called him after I woke shortly after midnight in an angered panic. The pencil portrait of Maisy had fallen to the floor next to my bed. I'd shuffled around in the dark on my knees trying to find it, while I dialed Dane's number. As the empty sound of his smartphone ringing had greeted my ear, I'd wept. I was grateful, in a small sense, when his voicemail picked up. I knew my emotions were too tangled for me to express everything I was feeling. I'd hung up without leaving a message. It was then that I finally scrolled through the missed calls on my phone, realizing that it had been my mom calling hours before. She'd left messages imploring me to call her back so we could choose a day for her to visit me and see my new apartment.

After I'd retrieved the portrait, I had taken it to the spare bedroom. I'd carefully placed it back on the easel and before I turned to leave the room, I'd given one last backward glance. Then, I'd shut the door behind me, knowing that the wooden door was not a strong enough barrier to ward off everything the drawing represented.

I'd climbed back into my bed then and somehow had tossed and turned in my sheets until sleep overtook me once more. When I opened my eyes again it was just past six. There was no return call from Dane and after I had a mug of hot coffee to awaken not only my body, but also my mind, I'd pulled in a deep breath and had called him again. This time, as the phone rang over and over again, I cursed each chime, wishing he would pick up.

I rest my thigh against the crib. "I tried last night and then before I came over this morning."

"Beck said you got here right before he left for his studio." She tips her chin in the direction of the ornate silver clock that hangs on the wall in Vane's nursery. "He's usually out of here around seven. What time did you get up?"

I don't need a reminder that losing sleep over a man isn't good for me. I know Zoe and right now, there's a lecture sitting on the very tip of her tongue. I didn't come here for that. I came here to escape the suffocating knowledge that the man that I'm falling in love with, neglected to mention to me that he's about to be a father.

"I got up early," I say in an effort to steer the conversation in any direction where the final destination isn't going to be Dane. "I went to bed right after you and Vanessa left."

"We left before eight," she points out. "You went to bed then?"

I couldn't face the world so I had done the only thing I could think of. It was the same thing I'd done when I was a child and I'd heard my parents contemplating the end of their marriage. The mention of my name had pulled me from the quiet solace of my bedroom and into the hallway. I'd listened intently as I'd stood out of their view near the corner that leads to the kitchen.

My father cried as he begged my mother to stay. There was no other man she'd told him. Her heart was empty and the passion that she once felt when she looked into his eyes was replaced with a friendship that was too quiet and comfortable. As I heard him beg her for another chance, she had broken down too and they'd sobbed in that small little house.

Neither of them ever mentioned separating again and just a few weeks ago, as they were both helping me recover, I'd caught them in a tender embrace in the hallway of my apartment. The storm cloud that had threatened their marriage had passed, and apparently, the bond they had forged after they faced the mutual realization that they may lose one another, was enough to cement their marriage.

"I wasn't feeling well," I mutter under my breath because I know in the scope of excuses, it's a lame one.

She bends down to pull Vane into her arms. "Vanessa didn't say a lot about Dane after we left your place. She doesn't know him as well as you do."

The irony of the statement isn't lost on me. I'm not going to assume that I know Dane better than anyone, including Vanessa. The tangible proof of that isn't just in the fact that up until last night, I didn't have a clear understanding of the depth of his connection to Maisy. It goes well beyond that.

Our relationship grew from a chance meeting in a restaurant when he was rushing away from a promised future while I was trying to find one. We haven't taken the time to discuss our deepest wishes and life goals. Up until yesterday, the thought of Dane being a father was a foreign concept. I certainly had never given it a moment of consideration in terms of what our future together might hold since we haven't even defined whether we're dating each other exclusively. The assumption that we are, is there, but talking about the direction our relationship is headed, hasn't hit my radar yet.

It obviously isn't something Dane thinks about because if it were, I would have known that a baby was in his immediate future.

"Why don't you go over to his place to talk to him?" she asks flippantly. "If I was dating a guy and I had questions about his past, I'd be out on his stoop waiting for him to get home."

I can't do it. I can't confess to my best friend that the man I'm seeing actually doesn't have a home because his pregnant ex-girlfriend is living in his. "I don't know his schedule this week. I'll stop by the fire station this afternoon."

The smile that floats over her lips is a clear signal that her only focus in this moment is her son. "That sounds like a plan, Bridge."

It's a plan, whether or not it's the right one, doesn't matter at this point. I want answers and the only person who can give those to me is the father of Maisy's baby who just happens to be the man I thought I was falling in love with.

# THREE

"I tried to call you twice but you didn't answer."

Dane's voice catches me so off guard that my left shoe lands firmly on the toes of my right one. I hadn't looked up at all as I walked quickly through the crowded streets of Manhattan. After I'd left Zoe's place, I'd tried to call Dane once more as I fidgeted in front of her building, while the doorman kept a watchful eye over me.

There wasn't an answer. I'd hung up just as his voicemail picked up before I'd tucked my phone back into my purse and started the hike from Park Avenue to the fire station Dane worked at. I kept my gaze far enough ahead of me that the possibility of locking eyes with anyone on the street was a non-issue. I didn't want to run into a regular patron of the pub who would pull me into a discussion about where I'd been for the past few months. I didn't have the emotional capacity to listen to another stranger tell me that they recognized me as the girl who had been hit by the police car. I had one focus that only intensified with each step I took and that was talking to Dane.

I couldn't hide the disappointment that swept over my expression when a man dressed in the same type of firefighter gear that Dane was wearing the night of my accident told me that he wasn't there. He tossed the words out in a breathless panic as he boarded the fire truck that was already pulling out into the street. I could only watch as it sped away in its pursuit to stop the destruction that only a fire can cause.

I'd walked back to my place, the fuel beneath each step a stirring mixture of anger and frustration. I didn't bother to look at my smartphone and as I rounded the corner to head up the block towards my building, I'd stopped to buy two apples and a chilled bottle of juice from a vendor who set up his cart in the same spot floors beneath my bedroom window each day.

I hadn't eaten before I'd left for Zoe's and although she offered me an omelet and some toast. I couldn't stomach the taste then. Right now, the fruit and juice is enough to tame the hunger pangs that I can't ignore any longer.

"Bridget," he says my name just as his hands reach out to grab my wrists to steady my balance. "I've been trying to call you for the last hour."

I stare up into his face. His features are exactly as they were the last time I saw him but there's something remarkably different in his stance. His shoulders are tense and pulled forward. His shoe is tapping against the pavement and as his skin touches mine I feel the tremor in his grasp.

"What's wrong, Dane?"

Just as swift as I see relief float over his face, it's gone again. "I know that you tried to call me last night and again early this morning. I couldn't get to my phone. I'm sorry."

"I wanted to talk to you about something," I begin before I look past his shoulder to a delivery truck that has pulled up next to the curb. The jarring string of horns honking a symphony of displeasure at the truck's driver fills the air. "It's really important."

"You want to talk about the fire, don't you?" His eyes dart back to where the truck is now parked. It's blocking a full lane of traffic on the already crowded street.

I want to talk about his son. I want to know if they've chosen a name for him and when Dane thinks his birthday will be. I want to know how he felt when he learned that Maisy was carrying his child and I want to hear him tell me, in his own words, what's going to happen when the baby arrives and what his plan is for every tomorrow after that.

"The fire?" I finally pull my wrists free of his grasp. "What fire?"

His eyes slowly scan my face as if he's searching for some semblance of understanding there. He's a fireman. It only stands to reason that he's talking about a fire he was called out to. I'm guessing it's the fire in Queens that Vanessa mentioned when she'd first arrived at my apartment last night. I assumed when she was hurriedly called back to the hospital, that it was because of that.

"It was bad." His hand darts up to his face to cover his mouth. "There were two kids. Their mom left them alone and..."

The audible gasp that escapes me stops him mid-sentence. I feel a rush of emotions as I remember the woman on the television who had been brought to her knees on the lush green lawn in front of one of the houses that was near the blaze. The wail that came from her had lingered with me and even this morning as I tried to catch a quick glimpse of the day's headlines on the muted television while I watched Zoe feed Vane his breakfast, I'd wondered about that woman and the loss she must have suffered.

"We tried to help them." His shoulders pivot towards me. "They don't know if they'll make it. I stayed at the hospital all night. Ben says it's touch and go."

"I'm sorry…I didn't…I had no idea that happened," I stammer, knowing that throwing a slew of questions at him about Maisy and his son will only add to the overwhelming emotional weight that he's already carrying on his shoulders. I don't want to feel compassion for him right now but I can't help it.

"I wasn't working the fire," he says quickly. "I was at my house and saw the smoke. I ran over there."

I know that the kindhearted thing to do is to ask about the children who were caught in the fire. I feel the tug at my heart as I think about small Vane and what it would do to Zoe, Beck and even myself if he were hurt. I want to stay in that place emotionally not only because it's the honorable place to be, but also because I despise myself right now for wanting to push his concern for those children aside to ask him why he was at the house he shares with the soon-to-be mother of his child.

"I know those kids, Bridget."

"You know them?" I whisper the question back, suddenly feeling guilty for not recognizing how completely torn up he is.

He scrubs his hand over his face. It does nothing to settle his expression. "They live a block over from me. They set up a lemonade stand every Saturday afternoon during the summer. I always take them a few dollars, when I'm not working, to buy a glass and talk to them. They're great boys."

I close my eyes against the flood of emotions I feel. My hand darts to my mouth. It's not because I feel a sob approaching. I need to physically stop myself from blurting out something about the little boy that him and Maisy are about to have.

"I don't know what I would do if I had a kid of my own and they got hurt." His voice turns gruff and takes on a raspy tone. "I sat with their mother all night at the hospital. She could barely talk. It's got to be hell to watch your sons suffering like that."

"Being a parent can't be easy." Taking a deep breath, I push all reason and compassion aside and say the one thing that has been there, tugging at me since last night. "You'll know that soon since you're going to be a dad."

# FOUR

We stand on the crowded sidewalk with the weight of my words sitting in the air between us. Dane's lips part briefly and I steady myself waiting for him to say something. I want to hear confirmation about the baby. I need to listen as he tells me about why he's kept that hidden from me since we met. That doesn't happen. As a group of pedestrians weave their way between us, Dane motions towards the door that will take us to the refuge of the lobby of my building.

During the elevator ride up to my floor, the scope of the conversation we are about to have is punctuated by the fact that a woman who lives in the same building as I, had called out to us to hold the lift as she raced through the lobby doors a few steps behind us, pushing a stroller where her bright eyed toddler sat. The little girl is happily pulling on two of Dane's fingers during the ride up, her mother apologizing the entire time for making us wait.

I feel Dane's hand on the small of my back just as I turn the key to unlock my apartment door. My first instinct is to pull away, but the gentle warmth of his skin against mine is giving me something I didn't know I needed. It's a reminder of everything that's transpired between us since that first night at the restaurant when he saved me from Larry's overly zealous grasp.

Dropping the items in my hands on a small table that's near the door of my apartment, I pull in a heavy breath. I hear the quiet click of the lock as Dane fastens it behind him.

I pivot on my heel to catch his eyes skimming carefully over my face. I look down, not wanting to give in to the temptation to accuse him of lying to me. By mere definition, the fact that he's about to become a father is something that he willfully chose to keep from me.

That might have made sense the night after his birthday when he came back to my apartment to fuck me. His past, and his future, didn't matter at all to me then. He was a man who I desperately wanted to share my bed with. I wanted to know the pleasure that he was capable of giving to a woman but once we started to share more of our lives, he made a conscious decision to not tell me about the baby. There's no excuse for that. You can't build a relationship on a foundation of lies, especially lies that will impact your life each and every day until you die.

"You're having a son." I get right to the point. "You're going to be a dad."

His gaze slides from my face down my body before his eyes level on mine. "Bridget."

I wait for more but I'm only greeted with the sullen silence that envelopes the space between two people who don't know what to say to one another. I can't stand the tension. There are countless things sitting on the edge of my tongue that I want to say to him. "What are you going to do about it, Dane?"

"Do about it? About my son?" he asks, his voice cracking with emotion. "That's simple."

No, it's not simple. It's a living, breathing human being who is part of Dane and will always be. There's nothing simple or straightforward about that. It's not supposed to be. Everything that comes with being a parent can't be put in a small box with a perfectly tied ribbon on it. Sometimes our choices in life have consequences that reach beyond today, tomorrow or even next year. We have to accept the hand we've been dealt and in Dane's case that includes raising a child with a woman who he doesn't live with anymore. It may not be ideal, but it is real and ignoring it won't make it go away.

"How is it simple?" I fight to control the anger in my tone. "Explain how any of this is simple?"

His large hands dart to his brow. He covers his eyes briefly before he looks over my shoulder and into my apartment. "It's a baby, Bridget. That's not complicated. It just needs love and care."

I smooth my hands over my hair, knowing that it must have taken on some curl from the humid air during my hike around the city earlier. "It just needs love and care? Do you think everything will just fall into place? You can't hide from something like this. You have to think about where the baby is going to live and who is going to have him during the week and who gets custody on the weekend."

"Custody?" His brows shoot up. "What does that mean?"

I don't need to define the word for him. He told me that Maisy's father is an attorney. It couldn't have taken more than a day or two after Dane ended the relationship before the issue of custody was tossed about. He's smarter than to play dumb with me. He's either trying to squirm his way out of our conversation because I've caught him so far off guard or he hasn't thought seriously about his own custody rights.

"Where will the baby live?" I push because I want, and deserve, to know what's waiting for him once Maisy gives birth. Even though I know that I was falling in love with him, I can't be with a man who hides such important parts of his life away from me. Beyond that, I can't fathom loving a man who tries to push his pregnant girlfriend out of his home right before she's about to have his baby.

His mouth thins. "I'll take care of it."

"You'll take care of it?" I seethe as I point my finger in the air towards him. "Time is running out, Dane. You need to start taking care of this now."

The air stills as he struggles to say something. He reaches out to touch me and just as his fingers brush against mine he drops to one knee in one swift, graceful movement. I don't have time to comprehend anything as I stare down into his tear filled eyes.

"Marry me, Bridget," he whispers the words as his hand clutches mine. "I love you. I'll love our son forever. Marry me before you have the baby so we can be a family."

# FIVE

I'm not one of those women who have sat for hours endlessly imagining the moment when the man I loved would drop to one knee and propose to me. I've never actually given it any thought. Marriage is something I definitely want but right now, the fact that Dane asked me to be his wife is only trumpeted by the reality that he told me he loved me and that he believes I'm having his baby. I'm not sure how I ran this conversation so far off the rails that he thinks I'm pregnant too but that ends now.

"I'm not having a baby." I pull on his hands trying to get him back to his feet. "I was talking about Maisy's baby."

He almost falls onto his jean covered ass as he scurries to his feet. "What? What did you just say?"

I repeat it all because I'm not sure which part of the truth he didn't catch the first time around. "I'm not pregnant, Dane. I know that Maisy is. I know she's having your son."

"You're not having our baby?"

I don't look up. I can hear the raw emotion in his voice. I don't know how he jumped to that as a foregone conclusion considering the fact that his ex-girlfriend is already pregnant. "I was talking about Maisy. I found out last night that she's pregnant."

"Wait." His voice is breathless. "Who told you she's pregnant?"

It's not an outright admission, but it's not a denial either.

"No one," I begin before I stop to adjust the hem of my sweater. "I met her weeks ago. Judging by how pregnant she was then, she may have already had the baby by now."

He exhales slowly. "You've never met Maisy. There's no way you've ever met her."

I fidget on my feet. "I met her the day before I met you. I mean I saw her. We never formally introduced ourselves."

His arms cross over his chest. "What? Are you talking about the day before I saw you at the restaurant? That was the day before my birthday."

It may be a stall tactic or it could be that he's genuinely looking for confirmation of the exact moment I laid eyes on his pregnant almost fiancé. "I saw the two of you at the museum that day. It was the MOMA. I was there drawing people. I drew her, but you already know that."

"Slow down." His hands dart into the air between us. "You're not making any sense. You didn't draw Maisy. It couldn't have been her. I can't remember the last time I was at the MOMA and Maisy hates art."

He's the one not making any sense. He'd held that pencil portrait in his hands when he'd been on my bed the first time I showed my work to him. I'd watched in silence as he'd studied that drawing in particular. It had struck a chord deep within me when I drew it and since his were the first eyes, besides mine, that saw it, I wanted to gauge his reaction. I'll never forget how his lips curled at the sides as his eyes slid over the paper. He'd lowered his head slightly as his gaze took in each fine line of the portrait.

"You saw the drawing," I begin as I motion down the hallway towards the closed door of the spare bedroom. "I showed it to you."

His eyes follow the path of my hand. "You didn't show it to me. I haven't seen it. Was it at the gallery?"

I tug on the small pendant that's hanging from a thin silver chain around my neck. "I didn't take it to the gallery. It's here. You saw it right after we met. It was on that night when you asked to see my drawings in my old apartment."

He scrubs his left hand over his forehead. "No. There wasn't a drawing of Maisy there."

I've only ever assumed that Dane is honest with me. Before yesterday I may have questioned the legal merit of Maisy's refusal to leave his house, but I'd never actually believed that he was consciously withholding the truth from me. Maybe that means I'm naïve and unaware or perhaps it just means that I wanted whatever we had to continue into my future so I chose to ignore the obvious signs that he wasn't being completely transparent.

I motion for him to follow me down the hallway. I don't look back as I take each step quickly until I reach the door of the spare bedroom. I push it open with a quick twist of my hand on the doorknob. I turn towards the easel where the pencil portrait is sitting near the window. "It's there. That's Maisy."

His eyes scan my face before he turns his attention towards the drawing. He takes a step in that direction and as he stops, his hands drop to his sides. I watch from behind him as his head tilts slightly to the left, before it moves to the right. "Are you talking about that drawing right there? Is it the drawing of the woman with the long dark hair? The woman in the wheelchair?"

I nod before I realize that he can't see the motion. "Yes. That's Maisy."

He pivots on his heel until he's facing me directly again. His brow softens as he looks down at me. "That's not Maisy. I don't know who told you that was her, but they're wrong."

# SIX

"Vanessa saw the drawing." I gesture towards it with a dip of my chin. "She told me it was Maisy."

He cranes his neck around so he can look directly at the pencil portrait again. "I have seen this. You showed it to me weeks ago."

"Why didn't you tell me then that it was Maisy?"

He turns back to eye me warily before he moves closer to the easel. His hands dart out to grab the paper, cradling it carefully. "I remember looking at this. You showed me other drawings that night. There was one of a woman outside a flower shop."

There might have been. I can't recall exactly what each portrait looked like. The only clear memory I have of that night is the expression on his face when he was looking at my work. He was entranced and when he'd told me that he thought it was gallery quality, it hadn't mattered that he was a fireman who appreciated art from the vantage point of a frequent visitor to the city's museums. At that time, his words meant more to me than any that even the most educated art critic would have shared.

My chest expands on a deep breath. "You looked at that portrait of Maisy back then and you didn't tell me it was her. Why didn't you tell me?"

"I didn't tell you because it's not her." He holds the paper in the air so it catches the early afternoon light that is streaming in from the window. "This isn't Maisy."

"Vanessa was sure it was Maisy."

"She's never even met Maisy." He shakes his head so slightly that the motion is almost unnoticeable. "I never introduced Maisy to her. My mother knows Maisy. My brother does too, but that's it."

*His brother?* The casual mention of a sibling I've never heard of only reiterates the reality that I know little about his life. I've never met any of his family beyond Garrett. I wouldn't know Dane's brother, or his mother, if I struck up a conversation with them on the subway. They're strangers to me, just as Maisy was until I saw her at the museum.

"Your mother was at the hospital with Maisy a few weeks ago." I try not to let all of the self-righteous indignation I'm feeling seep into the words. "Vanessa met her then. She saw them there together again two days ago. Vanessa said you were there too."

His jaw tightens. "My mother was with Maisy at the hospital? You're sure?"

I'm not sure of anything other than the fact that I feel as though I've fallen off a ledge into a bottomless pit of confusion. I don't know who to believe but I do know that Vanessa has never led me astray. She may view Zoe as her closest friend, but we've forged a bond the past few months that feels solid and secure. I doubt she'd willfully deceive me about the portrait. She saw Maisy in the woman's face in the drawing. Apparently, Dane doesn't see the same familiarity.

I tap my shoe against the floor. "I'm sure. That's what Vanessa told me."

His brow furrows for no more than a few seconds before he drops his gaze back down to the pencil portrait. He studies it intently as he mumbles something under his breath about the color of her hair and its length. "Did this woman have a mole under her eye?"

"A what?"

His fingers brush across the left side of his face. "Did the woman in the portrait have a mole under her left eye? A small mole? Was it there?"

I pull my hand to my lips as I lean forward to peer at the drawing. I hadn't included that detail. I had noticed it almost immediately but as I stood next to her and finished the drawing, I hadn't added the mole. Once I got home from the museum, I finessed the fine lines and then I'd slipped the paper into the cardboard box with the dozens of others I'd completed. I meant to add the mole, but I'd forgotten.

His words are less a question than a confirmation. He wouldn't know about the mole unless he knew it was there, adding to the beauty of her face. "Yes."

"She's pregnant?" he asks calmly. "You thought Maisy was pregnant because this woman is?"

I dip my chin towards the paper. "That woman told me she was having a son. She was there with a man. I just saw his back. He kissed her belly."

He swallows hard as he pulls in a deep, stuttered breath. "Was she happy? Did they look happy?"

"I didn't see his face," I begin cautiously. "I thought…I thought last night it was you there with her."

"It wasn't me." He eyes me carefully. "Did they look happy, Bridget?"

I nod slowly. "She was really happy."

His hand leaps to his chin as his gaze falls once again to the portrait. "She deserves to be happy. She deserves it all."

"Who?" I ask tentatively.

"Cleo," he says softly. "This has to be Cleo."

"I don't understand." I reach for the edge of the portrait. "Who is Cleo?"

"She's Maisy's sister." He slides the paper into my hands. "I've been looking for her for months."

# SEVEN

I stare down at the screen of my smartphone. I saw the resemblance between Maisy Trimble and her sister, Cleo, the moment Dane handed my phone back to me. He'd insisted on finding a picture of Maisy through an Internet search. It was a corporate headshot posted on the website of the financial firm she works at. I scan the details of her face before my gaze stops on her name. Mae Trimble. It's no wonder that Zoe and I couldn't find her.

"Her name is Mae?" I don't look up from the screen as I ask the question.

"She always hated that name." Dane's long index finger taps the edge of my phone. "Both sisters were named after their grandmothers. Cleo loves her name. Maisy has learned to like hers but she asked me to call her Maisy when we first met, so I did."

I study her face as I listen to the man she once loved telling me about her. It feels invasive and intimate in a way that I can't fully comprehend. I've never met her, yet now that I know that I spent a few brief moments with her sister, I feel a connection to her. Maybe that's defined within my relationship with Dane or maybe it's more about the fact that I no longer feel threatened by Maisy.

"We look nothing alike," I comment. "She looks completely different than me."

He chuckles softly. "Why would you look alike?"

"She's beautiful." I slide my fingers over the screen of the phone to enlarge the picture. "Her hair is brown. Her eyes are too. Most men have a type."

"You're beautiful, Bridget." He tugs on the edge of the phone. "I think you're the most beautiful woman in the world."

They may be words meant to placate me since I've just seen an image of his ex-girlfriend for the first time. I don't need that reassurance though. I've spent the night and most of this morning believing that Cleo was Maisy.

Cleo's smile is captivating. Her face is gorgeous and the glow that radiated from her may have been partially related to her pregnancy, but I have little doubt that it's always a part of her. She's everything that a woman could strive to be and when I thought she was Maisy, I didn't feel threatened. I only felt an obscure sense of gratitude to the universe that Dane had walked into my life.

"You said that you've been looking for her." I motion towards the portrait with my hand. Dane had set it back on the easel after he took my smartphone from me to find a picture of Maisy so I could compare it to her sister.

"I have been," he says quietly. "We had a disagreement."

"A disagreement?" I ask even though I'm not sure I have a right to know anything about Dane's relationship with Maisy's sister. I'm still basking in the relief I feel knowing that he's not having a baby with his ex-girlfriend.

His gaze roams over my face. "Maisy and Cleo had a disagreement. I was pulled into it. We lost touch after that."

In an age of smartphones, social media and email, it's hard to imagine anyone losing touch. There has to be more to it than Dane's letting on but I'm too exhausted and feeling too protective of myself to push. "I'm sorry to hear that. It seems as though Cleo was important to you."

"Cleo was like a big sister to me." He rubs his left bicep with his right hand. "She looked a lot different when I knew her. Her hair was shorter and blonde. She looks happy in that portrait."

"She was very happy."

He rakes his hand through his hair. "I'm glad. I miss her."

I don't respond because I'm unsure of what I could offer that would provide him any comfort at all. I have questions about what transpired between us just before he realized I drew Cleo. He dropped to his knee and proposed to me under the weight of what he thought was a shared child between the two of us. He professed his love for me and now in the shadow of all of that, his mind is focused on that delicate, yet strong, woman I met in the museum. It's a woman who is a part of his past, a direct connection to his last love and someone he obviously cares for deeply.

I may have gotten out of this with my relationship with Dane still intact but something tells me that now that he's gotten a glimpse into Cleo's future, he's not going to rest until he finds her.

***

"I know that you have a lot of questions." His lips flutter against mine. "I want to answer those."

I nod as I reach up to grab hold of the front of his blue dress shirt. "I need you to answer those, Dane."

His mouth finds mine again but this time the kiss is deeper, lush and fueled by more than a need to quiet my lingering doubts. "I wish I could stay and make love to you. I need to be inside of you."

My body may be craving the same thing as his but I'm grateful that he doesn't push for more. I tap my hands against his hard chest. "We'll talk soon and then we can be together."

The corner of his mouth slides into a smile. "I love being with you, Bridget. I want to be with you now."

I know that his need to touch me and feel my body against his is rooted in the fact that he's been through the emotional wringer this afternoon. Since he spotted me on the street, he's gone from believing that we were having a baby to learning that Cleo is.

"I need to get to work but I can come over tomorrow morning when I'm done."

I want to tell him that I'll be waiting for him but I can't. I may have escaped virtually unscathed from my mistaken belief that he was having a son with Maisy, but I feel beaten and battered emotionally. I need time to digest everything that he's said, and the things he hasn't said to me today.

"Why don't you call me after your shift?" I offer. "We can talk then."

He eyes me before he lowers his mouth to mine for one last, lingering kiss.

# EIGHT

"I'm sorry, Bridge," Vanessa says softly as she leans forward in the chair. "I honestly thought it was Maisy."

"I know." I tap the top of her hand with mine. "I saw a picture of Maisy. Dane found one online. She looks a lot like her sister."

She pulls her hand back to fumble with the edge of the paper coffee cup. "I know it was Maisy that I met here in the cafeteria that day. Dane's mom introduced us."

I'm tempted to ask how exactly Dane's mom, Anja, framed that introduction. Dane hasn't spoken that openly about his relationship with his mom other than to say that she's important to him. Judging by the fact that she was in the hospital with his ex-girlfriend for an appointment, I'd wager a bet that Maisy is still important to her.

"I guess that was Cleo I saw in the corridor with Anja the other day?" She furrows her brow.

I half-shrug my shoulder. "You're sure you saw them together? You said Dane was there too, right?"

I want to sound as nonchalant as I can about this. I had wanted to ask Dane about why his mother would be hanging out with his ex-girlfriend or her sister, but I don't have enough insight into his family dynamics to throw the question at him. I also didn't want to delve into the topic of Vanessa seeing Anja and Cleo with Dane until I could get confirmation from Vanessa. After I took Vanessa at her word about the portrait being Maisy, I realized that her perception may be skewed by the fact that she barely knows any of these people.

"Dane wasn't with them," she clarifies. "I saw him about an hour after I saw them. Actually, it could have been around the same time you have your appointment with Ben."

I feel relief wash over me. I remember that day vividly. Dane had kissed me in the bustling lobby of the hospital before I'd rushed to my appointment. It was only a few days ago in literal time but because of everything that's happened, it feels like it was years ago now.

"Did you know that Cleo was pregnant?" I stop to consider what I need to say next. "I was just wondering why you didn't mention that to me if you thought she was Maisy."

She leans back in the plastic chair pulling a faint cracking sound from it. "Cleo wasn't pregnant when I saw her the other day."

"You're sure?" I ask because I'm not a medical expert. I can't tell if a woman is six or eight months pregnant. I know that Cleo's belly was round enough to be visible once the blanket was pulled down but when I'd first started to draw her, I hadn't noticed it because of the oversize purse on her lap so it wasn't part of the finished portrait. The purse, she had been clutching in her hands, was there in the portrait.

"I'm absolutely sure," she chuckles softly. "We get a lot of pregnant women coming into the ER, Bridge. I know one when I see one."

***

"I'm looking for someone."

The woman sitting behind the reception desk pops her head up until her gaze meets mine. "What can I help you with?"

"Can you tell me if there's been a patient named Cleo Trimble admitted to the hospital?" I rub my hand over my eyes. I could have asked Vanessa to check for me but that would have only complicated things more. I didn't want to drag out our conversation about Maisy or her sister. I want Vanessa's focus to drift back to her upcoming wedding, not the complicated dynamics of Dane's ex-girlfriend's family.

"There's no one by that name registered." She doesn't look up from the computer screen in front of her. "Do you want me to try a different surname? Sometimes patients are admitted under the name that their insurance has listed."

I wouldn't know where to begin with that. When I saw Cleo at the museum her hand was void of an engagement ring and she spoke about marriage as if it would be part of her future. If she's not here under her maiden name, I doubt she's here at all.

"No, but thank you for checking." I scoop my smartphone into my palm from where I'd rested it on the counter before I turn to walk away.

"Wait." The woman behind the desk taps her fingers over her keyboard. "There's a Cleo Durand. Did your friend just have a baby?"

I should confess that she's not my friend. I should tell her that I'm on a fact finding mission that is only meant to quell my own desperate need to know more about the man I'm falling in love with but I don't do that. Instead I turn back towards the desk with a bright smile on my face. "That's her. She had a little boy."

# NINE

I stare down at the white, rectangular card in my hand. The woman at the reception desk had jotted Cleo's room number down for me. I'd walked away after thanking her in the direction of the elevators but before the lift raced back down to the lobby to pick me up, I'd darted out the hospital's main entrance doors.

I'd hailed a taxi then and during the entire ride back to my apartment, I'd contemplated whether I had any right to go see her. The woman doesn't know my name. It's highly likely that she won't remember my face either. Vanessa saw her without a swollen stomach which means that she's now a mom. A random woman who drew her portrait in a museum months ago is not someone she's going to remember.

If I'm being completely honest with myself, the only drive behind my desire to see her today was curiosity. She's Maisy's sister. She's also someone who is fundamentally important to Dane. She's not part of the fabric of my own life though and waltzing into her room, when she's just given birth to her first child, is not only selfish, it's also intrusive.

I turn just as I hear the faint knock on the door. I know it's him. He'd sent me a text hours ago asking if he could come over. I hadn't replied. It wasn't because I didn't want to see him. I longed to feel his arms around me and to hear his deep voice telling me again that he loved me.

My deliberate avoidance of him was wrapped up in that small card with the number 2049 written on it. He's been looking for her. I inadvertently found her and as much as my heart knows that I should hand him the card, my mind is causing me to pause.

Cleo is part of Maisy's life and even though Dane has been struggling with Maisy's refusal to leave his house since we met, I sense that there's a light of promise at the end of that tunnel. Guiding him back into the vicinity of Maisy's grasp isn't something I want to do.

I tuck the card into the front pocket of my jeans before I swing the door open.

"Bridget," he whispers my name as his arms circle my waist. "I was worried. You didn't answer my call or the messages I sent."

I fumble to find the right words. I pull back from his embrace to look up into his face. "You're wearing a ball cap. You look so young when you wear one."

"Young?" His brows shoot up. "How young are we talking?"

I push on his shoulder playfully. "You're one of the happiest people I've ever known."

He tugs the cap off his head before he rakes his hand through his messy hair. "I wasn't until I met you."

The concept of a man's words causing a woman's knees to go weak is real. I'm proof of that. I cling to the front of the dark sweater he's wearing. "You say exactly the right thing."

"I say the honest thing." He brushes his lips against my forehead. "You make me happy, Bridget. I live to make you smile."

I tuck my hand into the pocket of my jeans. My fingers fan over the edge of the card. "No one has ever made me smile the way you do."

"If I can put a smile on that beautiful face every day for the rest of my life, I'll die a happy man."

The words race through me with the power of a rushing wave. I reach for his shoulder to steady my stance. "I don't know what to say when you talk like that."

"You never have to say a thing." His right hand dips to my chin to pull my gaze up to his. "I can see everything you feel when I look in your eyes."

I tug my hand free of the pocket, lift it up to cup his cheek and I give in to my body's need to feel.

***

My hips involuntarily buck off the bed as he slides one of his long, firm fingers into me. I hear my own moan fill the quiet air in the room before I sense it within me. I close my eyes, not wanting him to see everything that I'm feeling. This time it isn't just about the magnitude of the pleasure that he gives to me. This time it's about the words he spoke when he kneeled in front of me. It's about the love that he feels for me.

"You're so wet, Bridget." His tongue dances over my clit. "I love how you taste."

I reach down to weave my fingers through his dark hair. I've never felt a need to direct the pressure or angle of his mouth on my core like I have with past lovers. Dane instinctively knows what I need. He can read my body better than I can and right now, I know that he senses that with just a few pressured licks of his skilled tongue on my swollen bud that I'll be racing over the edge towards an intense orgasm.

"Dane," I say his name not only to edge him on but to try to convey everything that I want to say. I wanted us to talk about his profession of love before we shared our bodies again. I wanted to hear my own voice saying it back to him. It's what I feel. It may be jumbled with confusion about his connection to Cleo or the lingering issues with Maisy, but my heart is bound to his. I know that now.

He buries his face between my legs with a soft sigh. His tongue races over my folds before he lashes my clit over and over again.

I don't want to cling to the edge of the sensation. I just want to feel and as the heat of my climax floods over me, I cry out from the sheer pleasure and the knowledge that this is the man I need in my life. This is the man I can't live without.

# TEN

"I love you, Bridget."

My eyes flutter open at the sound of his deep voice. I start to turn to face him but his chin is resting on my shoulder. His arms are draped around me, pulling my nude body into his. I can feel the pressure of his erection against my hip. After he licked me to orgasm, he'd crawled up my body and had kissed me with a fevered passion. I'd clung to him and as the tempo of our kisses quieted, he'd rolled me onto my back and had stared into my eyes before I started to drift to sleep.

"You love me?" I whisper as I try to crane my head to the side. It's not what I want to say. I want to flip over and tell him that I love him too. I want those words to flow from my mouth with the same grace as they did from his but I know that they can't. I know that if I say them now that they'll sound like an empty reflection of his confession. This is his moment. Mine will come, but it's not right now.

His hands grip my waist to guide me to turn over. I do it slowly knowing that once I'm settled next to him that I'll want to look into his eyes to see if I can find the same meaning within the words there that I hear in his voice.

I rest my hands on his bare chest as my eyes catch on the tattoo. It's a symbol of his love and adoration for his mother. She's the one woman who Vanessa saw with both Maisy and Cleo. I push the thoughts from my mind, wanting only to focus on what he just said to me.

"I said it the other day," he begins before he lowers his lips to brush over mine. "When I thought you were having our baby, I said it."

My heart drops slightly at the quiet admission. He had said it in the heat of the moment when he thought I'd just announced that I was expecting his child. I don't want him to back track and tell me that it wasn't grounded in his reality but in the momentary belief that we were going to share a baby boy. I study his face, my gaze sliding over his eyes. "I remember, Dane."

"On the street that morning I thought you were telling me that you were having my baby." He glides his lips across my cheek. "I was so happy."

I feel a stab of pure joy. "You were happy?"

He nods his head slightly, causing his hair to brush against my neck. "Having a baby with you would be a dream come true."

I hear the words clearly but absorbing them isn't as easy. A baby of my own is an abstract, but wanted, part of my future. I'm too young to even consider the notion of bringing another life into my world. My work is finally finding its audience and my heart has just started opening to this beautiful, caring man. A baby may be something we'd discuss years from now, after we'd traveled somewhere exotic on our honeymoon, and have shared a few anniversary dinners.

"I haven't thought about having a baby," I say honestly.

"I didn't either until I thought you were having ours," he murmurs in my ear. "It made me understand how much you mean to me."

"You said that you loved me when you thought I was pregnant." I graze my lips against his temple. "I understand if you said it because of that."

He pulls back so his gaze is on my face. His lips part just as his eyes lock on mine. "I said it because I mean it, Bridget. I love you."

I feel my lower lip tremble. Even if I wanted to repeat back the words to him, my body won't allow it. I'm tangled in such a tightly wound emotional knot that the only sound I can make is a tempered whimper.

"I'll say it again so you never forget it," he rasps. "I love you, Bridget Grant. I'll never stop."

***

My eyes catch on the leg of my jeans as I watch Dane pull the sweater he was wearing earlier back over his head. After he'd told me he'd loved me, he'd fucked me slowly, the entire time his eyes had held onto mine.

I had wanted to say those tender words to him but after we'd both came, he had kissed me deeply before pulling himself to his feet. He'd retreated into the bathroom and as I listened to the water from the shower running, I'd stood to stare out the window into the darkened city.

Everything I wanted was ten feet away from me, singing at the top of his lungs in the shower, yet I couldn't drag my feet across the small bedroom to join him. I wanted to but the weight of the words I can't yet say to him are there, tugging me back, making me retreat.

Now, as I watch him adjust the ball cap back on his damp hair, I know the moment is gone. I can't share my heart with him tonight. I can't do it with the knowledge that I'm the one holding things back from him.

"We need to talk about Cleo," he says as if on cue. "I want to talk to you more about her."

I reach for him as much to feel his touch one last time before he leaves, as to stop the urge I have to bend over so I can pull the white card with Cleo's hospital room number on it, from my jeans. I should have confessed to him that I know where she is. I should have told him that she's a mom now. I shouldn't have held onto all of that as he opened his heart to me.

He wraps me into his arms. "I'm so glad I came over. I have to go to work but I'll be back tomorrow."

I nod as I feel his lips rush over my cheek. Tomorrow. That's the day I'll tell him about Cleo.

# ELEVEN

"It wasn't Maisy?" Zoe holds up the carafe of cream. "Do you want some of this in your coffee?"

I shake my head slightly, holding my hand over the rim of the paper cup. "I don't have cream in my coffee."

"Right." She dips her chin down as she rips open the corner of a small packet of sugar. "Vanessa takes cream."

It's an off-handed comment that isn't supposed to sting as much as it does. Zoe's life is a balancing act. When she's not taking care of Vane, she's either in class at law school or working her way through her internship at an office in mid-town. The fact that she wanted to pour cream into my coffee is a gesture that comes from a helpful place in her heart. She can't know that it only punctuates the fact that she and Vanessa are closer than the two of us will ever be.

"We can sit over there by the window." I gesture towards a small, empty table next to two wooden chairs.

She tips the cup in her hand in that direction. "That's perfect."

I walk silently through the crowded café towards the table hopeful that by the time we reach it, another New Yorker hasn't settled there to read the morning paper or work on their laptop.

I skim the room as I take a seat at the table, waiting for Zoe to lower herself onto the chair opposite me.

"Vanessa said it was her sister or something," she says loudly as she blows a puff of air over the cup. She holds tightly to the base when she snaps the plastic lid back on top. "Did you even know she had a sister?"

I'm tempted to push back with a question about whether Zoe knows if the girlfriend that Beck had before they married had a sibling. Until a few days ago I didn't even know that Dane had a brother. I wouldn't label myself as informed when it comes to the important people in his life or the lives of the people he once loved.

"They look a lot alike," I offer. "I can see how Vanessa mistook Cleo for Maisy."

"Is Maisy in a wheelchair too?" Her face twists into a grimace. "That sounded insensitive. I didn't mean it like that."

She didn't mean it in any way other than curiosity. I know that. "Maisy isn't in a wheelchair. Vanessa saw them both at the hospital at different times. Maisy was sitting in the cafeteria and then she saw Cleo a few weeks later in her wheelchair."

"What were they doing at the hospital?"

It's a question I have absolutely no answer for. I've been meaning to ask Dane about his mother's relationship with his ex-girlfriend and her family but if I'm being honest with myself, the answer isn't something I'm sure I want to hear.

I don't have an ex-boyfriend who keeps in touch with my parents. Most of the boys I dated when I lived in Connecticut didn't even want to hang around my mom and dad when we were immersed in a relationship. I can't imagine any of them purposefully making plans to spend time with them. It's an abstract concept to me, but apparently it's not to either Maisy or Cleo.

"I think Cleo was there because she had a baby."

"How does that work?" She leans her elbows on the edge of the table. "I didn't know that women in wheelchairs could have children."

I didn't know either but it wasn't a conscious thought I had when I first realized she was pregnant. I didn't question the mechanics of how it was possible. I just reveled in the joy that had radiated from Cleo that day I met her. It was only a week later, after I saw another pregnant woman dining on a patio at a restaurant that the question crossed my mind. I'd meant to ask Vanessa about it back then but it didn't hold even importance for me to remember it.

"I don't know the details of her condition." I want to convey the sensitivity I feel. "It's something I want to talk to Dane about."

"Do you think he'll be open to talking about her?"

I haven't confided in Zoe since I left her apartment the morning that I thought Maisy was carrying Dane's son. It's not because I don't trust her with the complicated details of Dane's past. I don't want to cloud our friendship with all of the uncertainty I'm feeling.

I asked Zoe to meet me for coffee this morning so I could feel normal again, or at the very least, as normal as my life can be right now. I want to hear about her son, her job and I'm even hoping that she'll have a story or two to tell me about the people who live in her building. No one can gossip about strangers the way Zoe can. It's an escape from reality that I desperately need at this moment.

"I think he will be," I finally answer after taking a long sip of my coffee. "He told me he wants to talk about her."

"Get all the answers you need now, Bridge." She licks a drop of cream from below her lip after taking a drink. "Don't get closer to him until you know everything you need to about his ex-girlfriend and her family."

I stare across the table at her, knowing that it's the voice of experience talking to me. Zoe may not have faced the exact same scenario as I am when she first met Beck, but I sense she made certain that every skeleton in his closest was cleared out before she gave her heart to him.

# TWELVE

"I've been meaning to ask you something." I swallow hard past the lump in my throat. "It's about the night of the fire."

He pulls in a sharp breath. "The fire in Queens?"

I nod. "How are the boys that were in the fire?"

His gaze travels past my face towards the open kitchen of the small bistro we're sitting in. "They're both still in serious condition. I've been back to visit them at the hospital a few times."

I'm not surprised by that. I could tell, when he confessed that he'd been at the fire, that he was shaken to his core by the injuries the boys had sustained. I'd stopped at the bodega near my apartment one day when I'd noticed the newspaper's headline about the two boys along with a picture of their smiling faces. They'd both suffered smoke inhalation and burns to their hands and torsos. Dane was credited for helping to save them. I wasn't surprised in the least that he didn't mention the fact that he had raced into the house, along with several other neighbors, to carry the boys to safety.

"I hope they pull through." There aren't words that can properly convey what I'm feeling. I may not know the two youngsters, but any compassionate person would want them to recover so they can live the lives they're meant to.

A small smile tugs at the corner of his lips. "They're fighters. They've got a lot of support around them. The prognosis looks good."

"I'm glad," I say looking around the bustling eatery. Dane had asked me to meet him here because he wanted to grab lunch before he came over to my place. He already had ordered for us both by the time I arrived and now as I sip the lemonade the waiter brought for me, I realize that I don't have the small card that has Cleo's hospital room number written on it. It's still tucked deep within the pocket of the jeans that I tossed onto a chair yesterday after Dane left.

"Are you looking for someone?" he asks casually. "You seem nervous, Bridget."

I am. I didn't come here to eat half of the club sandwich he ordered for us to share. My stomach is doing so many flip flops at this point that I doubt I'll even be able to finish my lemonade. I need to ask him why he was at the house he shared with Maisy the night of the fire. It shouldn't be this difficult to form the question, but for some reason I feel as though I'm on the edge of a cliff that I don't want to jump off of.

"I'm not looking for anyone." I drop my hands into my lap. "I was hoping we could talk about your house in Queens."

"What about it?" He brings the glass of beer he ordered to his lips. He takes a large swallow while he watches me over the rim.

"Why were you there?"

His tongue darts over his lips to catch the last traces of the amber liquid. "I met a real estate broker there. I'm selling the place."

I'm relieved. It's the last tie that he has to Maisy and once it's sold it means he can move forward and find himself a new place. I skim my eyes over his face. I can see the disappointment that is there, hovering beneath the thin grin that covers his mouth. "I know that can't be easy. I sense that house meant a lot to you."

He blows out a puff of air between his lips. "I thought I'd live there my entire life. I had big plans for the place."

I don't want to let any jealousy seep into my response but I know, without any question, that part of those big plans involved his future with Maisy. She's not a fixture in his life now, and as soon as the house is sold, she'll be a memory that in time will slip from the forefront of his mind to a distant corner. "I'm sorry that you had to let it go."

He motions for the waiter to place the plate with the sandwich and a mountain of fries between us on the table. He thanks him quietly before he turns his attention back to me.

"It's just a house," he says casually although I see a hint of sadness in his eyes when he looks at me. "There are a lot of other houses."

I nod as I take a piece of the sandwich he offers me. "I guess this means Maisy found a new place to live."

His eyes close briefly as his shoulders tense. "Maisy is moving to the city. She's actually going to live with my mom for a while."

I feel like time stalls as the sandwich falls from my hand and bounces against the edge of the plate before it tumbles to the floor.

# THIRTEEN

There's an old saying about killing two birds with one stone. Talking about Dane's mom was the next thing on my conversation bucket list. I thought I'd clear the Maisy plate before I dove into the subject of Dane's mom's ongoing friendship with his ex and her family. Little did I know that Maisy and Anja are besties who are now going to be roommates too.

"Bridget," he says my name so softly that I have to strain to hear it. "Bridget, please don't get upset."

"I'm not upset," I toss back honestly. "I'm surprised."

"You're surprised?" he jokes. "Imagine how I feel."

I can't. I have no grasp on how anything that relates to Maisy makes him feel. I've seen brief flashes of anger and frustration when he's talked about her, but it's never gone beyond that. I've always assumed that he regrets parts of his relationship with her and wants her to become someone he once knew instead of someone who is still an integral part of his life.

"They must be close." I put my hand on the edge of the table. "Vanessa said they were at the hospital together too."

"My mom loves Maisy more than I ever did." He glances at me. "She assumed we'd marry and have kids. She's not letting go of that dream."

It explains a lot. I've wondered why I haven't met Dane's mom yet. It's not that I believe that we're at a stage in our relationship where that should be happening. The only reason he met my parents was because of circumstance. They were around a lot after the accident, and so it was inevitable that they'd get to know Dane.

It's different with Anja. She's based in Boston. Dane has told me that more than once. He's also mentioned that she comes to New York to visit him. "Did your mom stay with you and Maisy when she'd come to New York?"

He takes a big bite of the sandwich. Apparently the tension that is floating in the air between us does little to quiet his appetite.

His index finger pops up as he chews hurriedly. "She had her own bedroom at our place. Maisy helped her decorate it."

"Was she there a lot?"

"She'd take the train into the city a couple of times a month."

I adjust the napkin on my lap. "Is it hard for the two of you now? I'm just wondering if you two ever talk about Maisy?"

"We did the other day," he begins before he stops to finish the last of the beer in his glass. "She was there with Maisy when I went to meet with the real estate broker. She tried to tell me I was making a mistake."

"A mistake?" I parrot back. "Your mother thinks leaving Maisy was a mistake?"

"My mother thinks it's all a mistake." His hand flies through the air to circle the space above us. "She thinks I should have tried harder with Maisy. She doesn't understand how I fell in love with you. She wants me to keep the house and let Maisy live there. She thinks I'm just like my brother."

I pinch the bridge of my nose, as I feel a headache wash over me. Maybe it's just anxiety. After all, I just heard that the mother of the man I'm falling in love with is his ex-girlfriend's biggest fan.

Dane pushes the plate that is sitting between us aside. He reaches forward to grab hold of my right hand. "I love my mother. She's everything to me but she's wrong about this. You're the woman for me. Maisy and I didn't belong together and I'm nothing like my brother."

I smile at the faint grin on his face. "I thought my mom was difficult."

"I don't live my life for anyone but myself, Bridget." He brings my hand to his lips. "I can't make my mother happy. She wants to move to New York and right now she wants to live with Maisy. That's her decision. It has nothing to do with me and you."

***

"You're not going to invite me up to your place to show me your drawings?" He winks as the question leaves his lips.

"My drawings?" I cock a brow. "Isn't that some old pick-up line men used to use years ago?"

"If I had drawings, and a place to live, I'd use it only on you."

I throw my head back in carefree laughter. "There is something I should show you but I can't today. I'm meeting a friend. He's showing some of his stuff at a museum in a few weeks and they've agreed to include a few of my drawings."

"You're talking about Brighton Beck, aren't you?"

"I am," I say bluntly. "Do you know who he is?"

"He was at the hospital the night you were hit by the car." He cradles my cheek in his palm. "I knew it was him right away but I was too torn up over you to say a word to him."

"You like art." It's a statement, not a question.

"I've always liked it," he confesses. "I used to take Cleo to some exhibits before…"

"Before the disagreement?" I offer, wanting to move the conversation along. "What exactly happened between you and her?"

He reaches up the scratch his ear. "It's too complicated to get into now. It seemed like a big issue at the time, but now I realize I was wrong."

I don't push. If he wanted me to know, he'd at least give me a generalized account of what happened, without all of the pointed details. I can't ask for more than he's willing to give. "Disagreements have a way of fading away once time passes."

"I just wish I could talk to her again." He rakes his hand through his hair. "There's a lot I want to say to her."

I study his face. I only see compassion and goodness there. He may have fallen in love with someone who wasn't right for him and he may have to face the consequences of leaving her each and every time he speaks to his mother, but at his core, he's an honest man who has been nothing but loving and supportive to me.

"You can talk to her again." I tap his chest. "I know where to find her."

# FOURTEEN

"What is this?" He holds the small white card in his hands. "What is this number?"

I don't want to veil the truth of how I know where Cleo is behind any lie. I have to confess. "It's her room number at the hospital."

"Cleo is in the hospital?" His hands visibly start shaking. "Is she okay? What's wrong with her?"

For the briefest of moments before I pulled the card free from the pocket of my jeans, I wondered if his own mother had told him about Cleo since Vanessa saw the two of them together at the hospital. "She had her baby."

"She did?"

I don't know any details. I can't offer anything other than that card with the blue ink. "Vanessa told me that when she saw Cleo at the hospital with your mom last week that she wasn't pregnant. I asked about her at the reception desk and the woman working there told me Cleo was admitted. She actually called her Cleo Durand."

"Durand," he says the name softly. "She married David."

It's another name that holds no meaning to me. I feel the same emptiness that I did when he first mentioned Cleo a few days ago. These are people who are part of his past.

"David was one of Cleo's doctors." He taps the edge of the card against his palm. "He loves her so much."

"What happened to Cleo?"

His eyes dart up to my face as he shuffles nervously on his feet. "You mean why she can't walk?"

I nod, not wanting to give a voice to my curiosity. I've never known anyone in a wheelchair. I don't know the politically correct way to ask the obvious questions. I don't want to be insensitive but since I stood next to her in the museum that day, I've wondered how someone so bright and positive could find strength when her life is impacted in such a fundamental way.

After I'd left the museum and had walked home, I'd relished each step. I knew then and I still know now, that I was virtually unscathed after the police car hit me. My life could have been very different now and I doubt that I'd have the same grace and acceptance that Cleo does.

"There was an accident when she was an infant." He folds the corner of the card. "Her mother was holding her in her arms in the car. It was a short trip to the store. I think Cleo was four or five months old then."

It's true what they say about life changing in an instant. I listen, not wanting to interrupt.

"Her dad was driving and when they got home, he told her mom to wait so he could help her get out of the car," he pauses to look back down at the card. "She was in a rush to get inside so she opened the door and stepped out."

"What happened?" I ask anxiously.

"Her mom tripped." He shakes his head as if to ward off an image that is crossing his mind. "She dropped the baby on the concrete. She dropped Cleo."

I don't need to hear more. The medical details of how she was injured or the impact that it had on her development, don't matter. What does matter is that Dane is pulling me into his arms and right now, there's no place I'd rather be.

***

"I'll go see her tomorrow after my shift." He tucks the card into the back pocket of his jeans. "I need time to think about what I'll say."

Even though I've wrapped my arms around him and I've nestled my cheek into the soft fabric of the t-shirt that is covering his broad chest, I still feel as though there's a barrier between us. I want to offer comfort, or at the very least, understanding, but I don't know where to start. "Can I help? We can talk about it if you want."

"I do want to talk about it." He tenderly kisses my forehead. "As soon as I clear the air with Cleo, I want us to talk, Bridget. I want to talk about our future."

Our future? It's what I want to talk about too because a future with him is the one thing I want more than anything.

# FIFTEEN

"What would you say if I told you to move to Paris?"

"Bonjour?"

He cracks a wide smile. "You'd need to learn more than that. I can teach you the language. I speak fluent French."

Of course he does. Beck lived in Paris before he met Zoe. I didn't gather that tidbit of Brighton Beck's past from his wife or from his very detailed Wikipedia page. I got that from an article I read in one of the trashy gossip magazines I used to read when I lived in Connecticut and worked at the local supermarket. He moved there with one woman and ended up having an affair with another woman. I've never actually discussed that with Zoe because I want to keep our friendship in one piece. Bringing up her husband's playboy past would only hurt her.

"Why would I move to Paris?" I ask in my best French accent.

He cocks a dark winged brow. "Don't use that accent there. You'll offend the entire population the minute you open your mouth."

I pull my hand up to my lips to mask the giggle I can't contain. "I won't be offending anyone. I'm not moving to Paris. I live in New York."

"I went to Paris and my career took off."

No. He went to Paris and his libido took off. "You were famous before you went to Paris."

He tilts his head to the left. "I'm not famous."

I roll my eyes as much to make him laugh as to accentuate how ridiculous that statement is. "There's a graduate class at Yale that only covers your art, Beck."

He leans back and crosses his arms over his chest. "How do you know that?"

Zoe told me but not before I'd read about it myself. I've followed his career since well before I met him. He's one of the major players in the art world today. His water color paintings routinely sell at auction for six figures. He's gifted and humble enough to appreciate the talent of others. The fact that he runs a studio in the city that offers art classes to underprivileged youth is often noted in the press. He downplays it though and it's one of the reasons I strive to have a career just like his.

"I know a lot about you." I brush a piece of lint from my sweater. "I was a fan before you met Zoe."

"You were the only person in the pub the night I met her who knew who I was."

I had practically fawned over him. I'd rushed to get him a drink and when I brought it back I had hoped to launch into a rant about how much I admired him. My goal was to mention my own pencil drawings. I never had that chance because by the time I returned with his whiskey in hand, he was mesmerized by Zoe.

"Can I ask you something?" I approach a line of his paintings that are hung on the wall of his home office. "It's personal."

"You can ask me anything you want, Bridget." He moves so he's standing next to me.

"Zoe hasn't said a lot about your past relationships," I begin as I trace my finger over the edge of one of the canvases. "I read about some of them."

"There's a lot of information out there." He stares straight ahead. "Not all of it is accurate."

"Does Zoe know everything about your past?" I turn to look at his profile. "Have you told her all about it?"

I see a vein in his neck twitch. His brilliant blue eyes hone in on my face as he pivots his body to face me. "I've answered every question she's ever had. She knows that my life was empty before I met her. She knows that I love her more than anything."

"My boyfriend," I stop to consider the title. "Dane, the man I've been seeing, has a complicated relationship with his ex-girlfriend. She's close to his mother, and she has a sister that he cares a lot about."

"That bothers you?" He frames it as a question, not a statement which means I need to answer it.

"It worries me," I say honestly as I scratch the back of my neck. "It's like there are all these ties binding him to Maisy. That's her name. His ex is named Maisy. How can we be happy and together if she's still a part of his family and he's still part of her family?"

"Does he love you?" His hand darts to his stubble covered chin. "Has he told you how he feels about you?"

"He loves me." The sound of the words coming from my own lips stops my heart for a brief moment. "He's told me a few times that he loves me."

"Families are complicated," he says hoarsely. "Zoe's parents have never warmed up to me. It's not ideal but I love her and regardless of what anyone else feels, I'll never give that up."

Dane's situation isn't ideal either but he makes me feel things I never knew I could feel, and I'm not about to give that up either.

"Bridget." He taps his hand on my shoulder. "I'm serious about Paris. There's a three month internship program there that you're perfect for. I've already spoken to the director and there's a spot reserved for you. It would allow you to show your work in some of the city's most influential galleries."

"There are galleries here," I offer back. "I can build my career here."

"Promise me you'll give it some thought."

"I promise," I reply, even though the thought of moving that far away from Dane rips me to shreds inside.

# SIXTEEN

"I thought you came over to talk," I finally manage to say.

"I have been talking," he growls as he weaves his fingers into my hair. "I told you how good it feels when you suck me off."

He did say that. He probably said it more than once but I was too busy sliding my tongue over the length of the thick root to hear anything but the moans coming from deep within me. I'd brought him to the edge and just when I felt his body tighten, I'd pulled back hoping to be rewarded with a hot burst of his release on my lips. He'd managed to level his breathing enough that he held off.

His cock is still rock hard and as I graze my lips over the lush head, I hear a low groan seep from his mouth. "I want it to last, Bridget."

I do too. I actually want him to fuck me. My body is aching for it. I've wanted him to take me this way for days and when he texted me an hour ago to say he was coming over, I'd dropped my sketchpad on the bed in the other room and I'd taken a quick shower to freshen up.

I kissed him the minute he walked over the threshold into my apartment and he was quick to yank my clothes off before sliding out of the jeans and sweater he was wearing. Now, as he leans his back against the wall of my bedroom, I rest my cheek against his firm thigh.

"Lick it again." He pulls gently on my hair. "Let me see your tongue on it."

I shift back enough that I know that when he looks down he can see my mouth touching him. I slide my tongue over the head, stopping to circle it again and again. I wrap both my hands around the thickness, sliding them slowly up and down.

"Bridget." My name gets lost in a moan. "I need to fuck you now."

I have little time to react before his hands slide from my hair to my shoulders. He jerks me up, and in one quick movement, I'm on my back on the bed. He leans forward, his moist lips meeting mine in a sensual, deep and core touching kiss.

I reach up to grab his face but his hands are quicker than mine. He pushes them down, so they're resting on the sheets. "I have to put on a condom. Don't move. Don't move an inch."

I nod without a word. I pull in a deep breath as I watch him reach towards the nightstand to pull out a condom package. He rips it open without breaking our gaze. My eyes drop as I watch him sheath his erection quickly and deftly. His hand circles his cock, pulling the condom into place.

His eyes rake over my nude body. "You're so beautiful."

I blush at the compliment. I don't feel exposed when he looks at me. I always feel cherished and admired. My body may not be perfect in the eyes of many men, but I know when Dane looks at it, that he's seeing something he desires at the deepest level possible.

I cry out when he rams himself into me balls deep in one movement. I arch my back trying to adjust to the full length and girth of him.

"Take it," he whispers the words against my lips. "Feel it all."

I reach up to cup his cheeks in my hands. "I feel it. Please."

He starts moving. His hips pounding out a steady rhythm as his hands rest on the bed above me. With each pulsing thrust of his body against mine, a small growl flows from his lips. It's masculine. It's intoxicating and the sheer depth of him inside of me pulls my desire to the surface.

I clench myself around him, which only spurs him on more.

"Fuck," he says into the still air as he throws his head back. "Ah, fuck."

He pumps his hips into mine, each movement deeper than the last. I cling to his face, wanting to find my release so he can chase his own. I know he won't come until I do.

"Dane," I call out his name as I feel the rush approaching.

He adjusts his leg on the bed to gain leverage with his knee, curves his hand under my ass and drills his cock into me with a fierce tenderness I've never felt before.

I pull him closer as I feel the edge approaching and as I climax, I call out his name in a heated rush. He pumps one last time and through clenched teeth he lets out a low moan as he finds his own release.

# SEVENTEEN

"Did you see Brighton Beck about your drawings?" He pushes my hair from my forehead.

We'd collapsed into a mess of arms and legs after we both came. He held me for a few minutes before he pulled himself up, rid himself of the condom and went to get us a glass of water.

Now, he's sitting on the edge of the bed, completely nude. I stare at his back and the definition in the muscles. "I saw him. He thinks I should move to Paris."

His shoulders stiffen almost instantaneously. I watch as his hands leap to his face. "Paris?"

I reach up to run my fingers over the back of his neck. "There's an internship program there. They're saving a spot for me if I want it. Beck thinks it would help my career."

"It would." He turns briefly and I catch a glimpse of the side of his face. It's striking. I doubt that I'll ever tire of looking at him.

I adjust my body so I'm resting against the mattress again. "I'm doing well here. I'm still selling portraits at the gallery. I'm going to see if I can find people who want more commissioned pieces."

It's something I've been thinking about since I finished the drawing I did of Leanna Henderson. She loved it and Harper, the physical therapist who had helped me after my accident, even called to ask if she could buy her portrait. She was trying again with her ex and wanted to give it as a gift to him. I had dropped it off at her office with a smile and a question about her future. She was cautiously optimistic that they could make things work this time. I'd left her office with a hug after giving her the portrait as a gift.

"You're too talented not to chase your dreams, Bridget."

"I am chasing my dreams." I glide my legs along the soft sheets. "People pay to buy my portraits at the gallery and Brighton is going to include a few of my drawings in his exhibition. I'll be a featured artist he said."

He pivots his hips, pulling his knee up and bending it so he's sitting on the bed, half facing me. "There are more people in Paris who can help you. A lot of aspiring artists who go there hit it big."

I know he's only thinking about my future, but the fact that he's on board Brighton's one way train to Paris train surprises me. I want him to support my career, but I didn't think he'd be pushing me towards moving across the world. "Paris is far away."

"You have a gift." He turns towards the portrait I'd set on the dresser earlier. It's one I started earlier today when I spotted an elderly man in Central Park. "If you don't nurture it and go after every opportunity to share it with others, you're going to regret that one day."

I pull my arm over my face, trying to mask the disappointment I feel. "I can't move to Paris right now. I have too much going on here. I'm going to start back at the pub soon. They need me."

He leans forward, his left hand darting to the mattress to support his weight. His gaze catches mine as he looks down at me. "Nothing here is as important as your talent, Bridget. Think about this long and hard before you make a decision."

I turn away from him as I bury my cheek into the softness of my pillow. I don't know what there is to think about. Maybe the one thing that I thought was keeping me in New York isn't worth staying for after all.

***

"I think you should take that portrait you did of her to the hospital and give it to her." Zoe motions towards the portrait of Cleo that is still sitting on the easel by the window.

I glance towards it. Since I found out that it was Maisy's sister I've been able to walk past it without feeling as though my heart is dropping out of my chest. "I don't know her. I don't think going to the hospital is a good idea."

"Why not?" She pulls a portrait I did last year of a couple from the cardboard box that is now sitting atop the bed. "I think it would mean a lot to her."

I've thought that too. I've never drawn people as a means to financial gain. I've been lucky that my portraits have sold as well as they have but I've always felt it would have more meaning if I could hand some of them back to the people I captured with my pencil. Cleo is a perfect example of someone I drew at a pivotal time in her life. She was pregnant, planning her future and celebrating with the man she loved.

"I need to talk to Dane about it first." I reach past Zoe to rifle through the drawings. "Beck said I should pick portraits for the museum that would speak to a lot of people. He wants me to choose some that mean the most to me."

She nods as she begins pulling more from the box. "If you don't take Cleo's portrait to her today, she's going to be discharged and you'll lose your chance to give it to her."

I turn back towards the window and the drawing. "I'll text Dane first and if he's okay with it, I'll take it."

I'm grateful when she doesn't respond. I know she's aching to tell me that I don't need Dane's permission to do anything, but when it comes to Cleo, I don't want to get in the way of him trying to mend the friendship the two of them once had.

# EIGHTEEN

"Visitors are only allowed for another hour." Vanessa glances at her watch. "My break is then, so go see her and then I'll buy you some dinner."

"Cafeteria dinner?" I joke. "I might pass on that."

She elbows me in the ribs. "It's not that bad. I eat it all the time."

"I can't tonight," I say honestly. "I'm starting back at the pub. I need to be there by nine."

"We can do dinner another night then."

I look down at my smartphone again. I had texted Dane to ask if he could call me. That was more than two hours ago. I know that he told me when his schedule changes this week, but I hadn't paid attention mainly because I was drifting into a dream at the time.

I could have waited until tomorrow to come to see Cleo to bring her the portrait, but after considering what Zoe said, I don't want to miss my window of opportunity. My plan is simple. I hand her the portrait, tell her that I saw her in the hallway and I leave with no mention of Dane.

"You remember her room number?"

"It's 2049." It became etched forever in my memory after I'd glanced at the card so many times. Cleo is my first link to Dane's life beyond his cousin, Garrett. She's his friend, or was at one time. She's also the sister of the woman he once loved. I want her to have the portrait. It belongs to her.

"If it's too hard, come find me." She wraps her arms around my shoulders so tightly that the stethoscope hanging around her neck pushes into my chest. "Send me a text and I'll come up to the second floor."

I hug her back. This might be the biggest mistake of my life or it may be a kind gesture that Dane and I will think back on when we're reminiscing about our past. It doesn't matter at this point. I'm here now and I'm not leaving until the framed portrait in my hand is nestled securely in Cleo's grasp.

***

"Excuse me."

The voice is softly feminine. It's also behind me just as I'm about to walk into Cleo's room. I'd peered through the rectangular window in the door but the only thing I could see was a light blue curtain drawn around a hospital bed. There's a wheelchair near the foot of the bed so I can only assume that I'm not too late.

I ignore the voice when I realize that she's likely talking to one of the many other people who are walking through this corridor. I've passed at least two doctors and half a dozen nurses since I exited the elevator on this floor. It's the maternity wing of the hospital which means most of the people who work here are less frantic and rushed than those who work in the ER with Vanessa.

I place my fingers around the handle as I hold tightly to the portrait that I'm cradling against my chest.

"Wait." Her voice is louder now. "You're Bridget."

She's talking to me. I push through my memories for any familiarities in the voice but there's nothing. She must have seen my picture in the newspaper or online after the accident. I've learned, since that night, that some people are morbidly curious about those who are struck by bad luck.

Since I'm intent on getting into Cleo's room without this woman in tow, I need to ditch her now. I turn quickly and the moment I do I'm struck by how attractive she is. She's tall, dark haired and even though her face is bare from make-up and her eyes rimmed with glasses, her natural beauty is still there.

"I'm Bridget." I reach out my free hand towards her.

"I know." She scoops my palm into her right hand, before covering it with the left. "I'm Maisy Trimble."

# NINETEEN

"This is Cleo." The frame balances on her knees as she runs her hand over the glass. "You drew this?"

I nod. Since we'd exchanged pleasantries outside of Cleo's hospital room, Maisy had asked me to join her in the family lounge. It's a quiet space, tucked into a corner beyond the patients' rooms. Her sister had fallen asleep, she told me. It wasn't a good time to visit.

"I saw her and her husband at the museum one day," I offer as I reach to touch the edge of the frame. "I didn't know who she was then."

"Was this before you met Dane?"

She says his name with such effortless ease that it catches me off guard. There's no anger or resentment woven into the question.

"It was before then," I answer quietly. "I didn't know who she was until a few days ago."

"I wasn't talking to her then." Her hand skirts across the glass. "She's beaming in this. Did she know that you drew this?"

"Yes." I work to contain my emotions. "She called me over and we talked."

Her lips curve into a bright smile as she looks up and at me. "What did you talk about?"

I pull back slightly, wanting to gain some distance. I'm still emotionally stuck back in the corridor when I realized who she was. I've been staring at her since we sat down. She looks softer in person than she does in the online profile picture Dane showed me.

"She talked about getting married, and going on a honeymoon."

She studies me. "It's ironic, isn't it?"

Lifting my head I look across the empty room. "What's ironic?"

"That we're sitting here together."

It's not so much ironic as it's wildly uncomfortable. She may not have come right out and told me directly that she knows I'm dating her ex-boyfriend, but the knowledge of it is there. I have no idea who told her. It may have been Dane. Perhaps it was his mother or his brother. It doesn't matter at this point. What does matter is that I'm sitting next to a woman that Dane loved enough to live with. There has to be something about her that struck a deep chord within him.

"The world is a small place." I reach for the edge of the portrait. "It was inevitable that we'd meet at some point."

"Inevitable?" She glides the frame back into my lap. "Why would you say that?"

"We both loved the same man," I say it quietly. "You loved him. I love him now."

The silence that fills the room is finally broken by the sound of a man's voice from the corridor. "Bridget, I need you. Come with me, now."

***

I've never sat in a chapel in a hospital before. It's a place that I've always felt was reserved for those who lost a loved one or those who craved the comfort that they found in whispering their prayers of hoped healing to a spirit they believed in.

I'm sitting next to Dane now and as he crushes my fingers within his clasped palm, I feel the weight of a loss on his shoulders. He hasn't told me what brought us here. We didn't talk as he guided me down the corridor with his hand around my waist.

I'd left the portrait of Cleo with Maisy. Her presence outside the door of her sister's room made it clear that whatever strife may have pulled them apart was gone now. Maisy had been there for hours. I could see it in her face and by the wrinkled clothing on her back. She had come there for her sister and when I walked away, I knew that if Cleo had found it in her heart to forgive Maisy, forgiveness for Dane must be there too.

"What happened?" I pause. "Do you want to talk about it or do you just want to sit?"

He lowers his head just enough that his lips are out of my view. "People think I'm selfish."

They're not the words that any woman wants to hear when she just met the ex-girlfriend of the man she adores. I didn't consider the fact that Dane may have spent the past few hours in this hospital, engaged in a conversation with Maisy.

Maybe she stumbled on me first as she headed back to her sister's room and Dane was close behind. Perhaps that's why he pulled me from that room so he could break my heart here, where people come to seek solace in their grief.

"You're not selfish." I try to derail his train of thought. I know it's foolish and only a temporary reprieve from whatever he's about to tell me but I don't want this to end. I love him and if he walks away from me before I've had a chance to tell him, I will regret it until I take my last breath.

He swallows hard. "Maisy's mother is ill. That's why my mom is moving here temporarily."

He can't leave me because the mother of his ex has gotten sick. That's a situation that's not his to handle anymore. "I'm sorry to hear that."

"They got close after Maisy and I introduced them to each other." He taps his foot against the grey tiled floor. "They email each other a lot and they skype. My mom loves her mom."

It's another thread that weaves his life back into Maisy's. "Did Maisy tell you about her mom?"

"We had coffee earlier." He doesn’t look in my direction at all. "I came here to see Cleo and after we talked, Maisy showed up."

I was too late. I'd taken too long to get here and because of that, Maisy had cast her net out and captured him again with the bait of her mother's sickness. It's a horrible way to think and I feel instant guilt for it, but I'm sensing him pulling away and since he's the only man I've ever loved, I'm going to fight for him, even if right now that seems futile.

"My mom has been coming to the hospital to see Rhona. That's Maisy's mom."

"Why didn't your mom tell you she was sick?" Maybe it's an insensitive question but it's a valid one. He's told me repeatedly that his mother feels a special kinship to Maisy so it only stands to reason that she'd feel the need to share Rhona's illness with Dane since he was once part of her family.

"My mother told me." He pats the front of his shirt where his phone is tucked into the pocket. "She called me a few weeks ago to tell me and I told her it was Maisy's problem."

It is her problem. That may be the crass approach to take but no one can expect him to drop everything in his life to cradle his ex-girlfriend because she's facing a crisis. "Your mom is helping. Maisy seems strong. I'm sure they can handle it."

"I haven't been there for my mother." His hand slips from mine and I feel lost instantly. "I've pushed everyone aside to take care of myself. That's not who I am, Bridget. It's not who I want to be."

# TWENTY

We sit in silence, the only connection between us the side of our thighs as they touch. Soon after Dane dropped my hand, a young couple came into the chapel, clinging tightly to one another as they'd wept on their knees at the altar.

Dane had twitched slightly when we heard them talk about funeral plans and calling relatives they hadn't spoken to in years. It was an intimate view into the mourning process of two people we'd never see again.

"I want you to meet my mother," he whispers softly.

"You what?" I ask feeling embarrassed that I thought the next words out of his mouth would be that we needed to take a break while he dealt with the family he already had.

He glides his palms over the legs of his jeans. "I need you to meet my mother. I want her to see you. I want her to know you. I wish that could happen."

I want that too. "I'd like to meet her."

"I've told her all about you." He leans towards me to rest his forehead against mine. "I told her how amazing you are. She knows how talented you are."

I close my eyes against a surge of emotions. "I didn't know that you talked about me to her."

"That's all I talk about when she calls." He shakes his head slightly. "I sent her some pictures of your portraits. She read about the accident."

I glance down at where his hands are clasped together into a fist on his lap. He's trying to edge me into feeling secure in the knowledge that he's told his mother about his love for me but I know that she still views his leaving Maisy as a mistake. He told me as much just a few days ago.

"Your mother wants you to be with Maisy." I don't say it out of spite or jealousy. I say it to remind him that when it comes to his mother's acceptance, it's an uphill battle I may never win.

He rubs his hands over his face. "I have a brother. Landon. He's thirty-two."

"You have an older brother?" I purse my lips together. "You mentioned once that you have a brother."

"I never see him anymore." He scowls. "My mother doesn't either."

"Why not?" I push. I want a clear understanding of his family dynamic.

He looks towards the couple who are now sitting on one of the pews a few feet away from us. "He's a pilot. He's always away. When he's in New York, he's hanging out with whoever he met the night before. He shows up during the holidays for a drink or two and then he's gone again."

I glance past him to the clock on the wall. It's well past the time I was supposed to be at the pub. I can tame Elliott's anger tomorrow. Tonight, Dane needs me and if I'm being completely honest with myself, I need him too. After seeing Maisy, I'm shaken to my core.

"My father died when I was a teenager so I'm all that my mother has left."

Shock pulses through me. Although he never mentioned his dad I hadn't made the assumption that he was no longer in Dane's life. "You've never told me that."

"I hate it." He closes his eyes on a heavy swallow. "I need him. I miss him and every day I wish I could talk to him one last time."

I think about my own father and the deep sense of loss I would feel if I couldn't dial his number and know that he'd pick up with a cheery greeting at any time day or night. "I'm sorry you lost him."

"My dad would have loved you, Bridget." His hand scrubs the back of his neck. "He would have fucking loved you just as much as I do."

***

"Can I come home with you tonight?"

I pause to look over at him. "You want to come back to my place?"

He licks his lower lip as his eyes skim over my face. "It's the only place I feel like I belong anymore."

My breath catches and the fact that I audibly gasp gives credence to everything I'm feeling.

His lips hover next to mine as the couple who had sat in the pew, stand to take their leave. "Don't be scared, Bridget. I'm not going to push you into anything. I just want you to know what I feel."

"You can come home with me." I hold out my hand. "You can stay all night and tomorrow we can talk about what's next."

"I already know what's next." He places his large hand over mine, completely covering it in its embrace. "We both do."

# TWENTY-ONE

I wake just as the morning light breaks through the slim space that separates the ill fitted curtains that cover my living room window.

After we'd come back to my place, Dane had helped me into the shower and as he'd silently washed my hair and body, he'd stared at my face. I didn't ask him what he was thinking. I just stood quietly with my eyes locked onto his.

He'd carried me to my bed after that and had kissed me until I was dripping wet with want and need. He'd slid his body into mine then, without any protection. I hadn't stopped him. It was an act of trust and commitment that we both wanted and since I've been taking birth control pills on and off for years now, the risk is low.

We'd fallen asleep in each other arms until I felt his lips against my back shortly past midnight. His greedy hands fell to my breasts and as he massaged one nipple between his strong fingers, the other hand slid to my core. I'd come quickly and loudly, falling into his chest before he picked me up and carried me into the living room.

He'd sat me on the couch then and handed me my sketchpad and a pencil.

"Draw yourself for me, Bridget."

They were the only words he spoke and as he sat next to me, with the light that was cast from a single lamp on the table, I'd drawn myself for the first time.

His breath raced over my neck as he leaned in to kiss my cheek to thank me and as I turned to him I saw a flash of something I'd never seen before in his expression. It might have been weariness from the emotional toll that the day had taken on him but as I studied his deep brown eyes, I saw a need there that only I could satisfy.

I'd slid the sketchpad onto the sofa next to me and had crawled into his bare lap. As I sat there, with the heat of his arousal pressing into my core, I'd held his strong and handsome face in my palms.

He tipped his chin slightly as if he was coaxing me forward and just before my lips touched his, I said the one thing I'd longed to say to him for weeks. "I love you, Dane."

His hands found my hair and as he curved his lush lips over mine, he whispered the words back into our kiss.

We fell asleep again then, resting on the narrow couch with our bodies pressed against each other.

Now, hours later as my eyes adjust to the space, I scan it looking for him.

I dart to my feet as soon as I notice the page ripped from the sketchpad. I stumble past the coffee table and down the hallway to my bedroom. My hand jumps to cover my eyes as I flick on the light switch in the bathroom and my heart sinks when I realize that the clothing he discarded there, on the floor, last night is gone.

I race back towards the living room, in search of my smartphone but my eye catches on a white envelope perched on my bed. It's resting against the headboard as if it was placed there with a sense of care and thoughtfulness.

My name is written in messy handwriting across the front and as I reach to pick it up, I sob. I know what it's going to say. I know that the message won't be about love that withstands life's trials and tribulations. It won't be a declaration that promises me endless tomorrows.

I flip it over and run my finger under the flap.

I reach into the envelope to pull out a folded piece of white paper. I feel my knees buckle as I lower myself to my bed.

I smooth my hands over the paper wanting to soften the creases. It's a printed confirmation of an airline ticket in my name. It's one –way from JFK to Paris, leaving two days from now.

I pull open the flap of the envelope wider and spot something else. It's a piece of paper taken from the stack that I keep on my kitchen table. It's the ripped corner of a magazine and written across it in black, bold ink are three simple words.

**Go to Paris.**

I drop it all on the bed as I pull a dress over my head before I slide my feet into a pair of sandals, grab my keys and phone and race out of the door of my apartment.

# TWENTY-TWO

"Dane?" I say his name softly because I don't want to wake her.

It's early. Visiting hours only began ten minutes ago. I'd waited in the lobby of the hospital until the woman behind the reception desk told me I was allowed to go up to the second floor to Cleo's room.

I'd raced around New York looking for him. I'd stopped at the fire station first and when I stepped up the driveway towards the doors that shield the large red trucks from the street, the same fireman I saw a few days ago, came towards me.

Dane had been there, he told me. He was his captain and Dane had talked about me. He knew I was the artist and an hour before when Dane walked into the station to request a three month leave of absence; he hadn't hesitated at all when he gave it to him. Dane's job was waiting for him as soon as he returned from taking care of whatever he needed to tend to.

He'd read Dane's home address from the personnel file that was already on his desk. I punched the numbers into my phone before I ran out of the station, rushed to the subway stop and boarded the train. I sat on the worn seat tapping out a text message to him about needing to see him. I stared at my phone the entire ride, waiting for a response, but there was nothing.

Once the train stopped, I asked for help. A kind man with green eyes waved his arm in the air towards the taxi line on the street. I'd need to take a cab to the house but the fare shouldn't be more than ten dollars he told me. I squeezed his forearm in thanks.

As the taxi pulled up to the curb, I saw the sign. SOLD it said. I asked the driver to wait while I opened the small white wooden gate and walked up to the front door. I knocked, before pressing the doorbell but no one answered. He wasn't there. Maisy wasn't there and when I peered through the open curtains that were meant to hide the front parlor from the view of those passing on the street, I saw empty rooms. Whatever life he'd built in there with

Maisy had been cleared out. All that was left was a vacant space, ready for the new owner to arrive to fill it with a different life.

I slid back into the rear seat of the taxi and asked the driver to take me into Manhattan. I knew where he'd be and wasting time waiting for the subway wasn't worth the cost.

I had to get to him and now as I stand in this quiet hospital room and look at his face, I see something I didn't see in the note that he left.

"You're coming to Paris with me, aren't you?

"I'm already packed."

I move towards him and in an instant his arms are around me. He buries his face in my neck and just as his lips slide across my cheek, I sense her presence. I turn and that's when I see the same beautiful face that I did in the museum. She's awake. She's smiling and just as she nods her approval, Dane kisses me softly.

***

"My sister showed me the portrait."

I skim my eyes around the room but all that I find are two bouquets of wilting flowers and a few greeting cards that have fallen over from the pressure of the air conditioning blowing on them. "I wanted you to have it."

"My husband took it home." She motions towards the door of the room with her finger. "I asked him to hang it in the baby's nursery."

I'm touched by the admission. I wanted the portrait to mean as much to her as it had to me.

"The baby is named Davey," Dane interjects.

"It's David, actually," Cleo corrects him with a smile. "We named him after his father."

Dane taps his hand against the top of the bed near where her feet are covered with a thin, blue blanket. "Everyone is calling him Davey. It's what I'm going to call him."

Cleo smiles as she reaches her hand out to grab his. "He'll like that. You'll come to see him when you get back from Paris?"

The words jar me even though he confirmed right after I'd walked into the room that he was going to move there with me. He's putting his entire life on hold here, to help me follow my dream.

"I'll send him postcards," he says. "Maybe a few presents too."

They speak to each other as if they're old friends. Anyone walking into the room right now would never suspect that something tore them so far apart that they didn't speak for more than a year.

"Having you here makes everything right again, Dane." Her eyes float from his face to mine before they settle on his again. "I told you Mae wasn't right for you. I knew there was someone perfect waiting for you out there."

The words catch my heart in my chest. I lean back in the weathered vinyl chair that is next to the bed. Dane looks at me for only a brief second before he slides himself closer to Cleo. "You were right. At the time it hurt Maisy when you said that. I cared about her so it hurt me too, but you were right."

"It more than hurt her." She rests her head back against the pillows. "You both stopped talking to me because Maisy thought I was jealous of your relationship."

This is the conflict that tore Dane from her life. It wasn't something catastrophic. It had nothing to do with hatred or spite. It was an older sister trying to save her younger sister from eventual heartbreak.

"I knew when I met Bridget that she was the one." He taps his fingers against my knee. "I love her more than my heart is capable of."

"That's exactly how I feel about my David," she stops before she swallows hard. "And now, my little David too."

"You'll be home with both of them soon." Dane rubs his hand over his brow. "When can you be discharged?"

"I need extra care." She dips her chin towards her stomach. "I had no idea that a caesarian section would be this rough."

He leans forward to kiss her softly on her forehead. "You're the strongest woman I've ever met. Give it some time and you'll be home holding that little guy in your arms."

# TWENTY-THREE

"I'm going to learn French."

I stare up and into his face. "That's your plan for when we're in Paris?"

"I'm going to Paris to watch you shine." He presses his chin into my hair. "It's a vacation for me. It's an adventure."

"An adventure?" I glide my hand from my lap onto his thigh. "When did you decide that we were going to Paris?"

"The day you told me about the internship."

I snuggle closer to him on the bench. It's mid-morning and after he'd said goodbye to Cleo, we'd walked out of the hospital hand-in-hand. We didn't have a clear destination and as soon as we walked into Central Park and saw the vacant bench, we both motioned towards it at the same time.

"You're giving up a lot to go there with me." My voice is laced with not only appreciation, but awe.

Adjusting himself, he crosses his long legs. "You would be giving up more by staying here and since I can't be away from you, I need to be there. I have to go with you."

We haven't spoken about the financial aspects of a three-month move around the world. The internship offers a small monthly stipend, which includes housing for me and my companion. I have enough saved to cover meals and transportation but I doubt that Dane will stand idly by while I pull out my wallet each time we go to a café or purchase a bottle of wine.

"You'll live with me in the housing they provide, won't you?" My heart races a little as I ask. It's obviously the most economical way for us to be together there but it's also a major step in our relationship.

His arm tightens around my shoulder. "We'll live together. I'll help you with all your other expenses. I'll cook for you and every day when you're done at the art school, I'll be waiting outside the door to walk you back to our place."

"I can cover a lot of the expenses," I say sheepishly. I have no idea what his salary was at the firehouse. I know that since he won't be working for the next few months that he'll be dependent on his savings for necessities. I'm not about to allow him to eat through that so I can follow my own life's dream of being an artist.

"Bridget." He cradles my hand in his as he brings it to his lips for a soft kiss. "Maisy and I came to an agreement."

"An agreement?" I don't feel an ounce of hesitation as I ask. It's different now. I've met Maisy and that has given me insight I didn't have a day ago. She's not the evil, self-centered creature I conjured up in my mind. She's a woman. She's just a woman who loved Dane once.

He sighs. "She wouldn't leave the house because she didn't want to give up her investment in it. She admitted last night that it was because she was pissed at me for leaving. I knew it. It was obvious but I'm glad she finally gave up."

"I know the house was sold."

"You do?" He tips my chin back with his hand so he can look at me directly. "How do you know that?"

"I went there this morning," I admit with a weak grin. "I took the subway to Queens. It's a nice house, Dane."

"It sold within hours after it was listed." A ghost of a smile pulls at the corner of his mouth. "I kept everything looking great when I lived there."

I reach up to touch his cheek. "I can see why you loved it."

He straightens his back. "It was my home but it's sold now and Maisy agreed to take a small percentage of the sale price. I wanted her to have that. We shared expenses and at one time it felt like our house, not just mine."

I give him an empathetic nod. It's the last chapter in a love story that didn't have a happy ending. They're parting on good terms and with respect for each other which is more than many couples have when their love dies.

"I'm going to investment most of that money but I'll use some for our Paris adventure."

My heart is pounding as I look up into his dark brown eyes. "We're really going to do this?"

"We are," he growls. "We're going to start our life together there, Bridget. It's the life we were always meant to have."

I smile as I reach up so his lips can find mine for a kiss that speaks of the promise of every tomorrow that awaits us.

# EPILOGUE

***Three Months Later***

"Your landlord hasn't rented out your apartment while you've been gone, has he?" He leans back onto the sheets of the bed. "We have a place to live in New York, right?"

"Maybe," I tease with a serious expression and a half-shrug of my shoulder.

He cocks a dark brow before running his hand over his beard. "What does that mean?"

"Have I told you how young you look with that beard?" I stroke my hand across his jaw. "I like it a lot."

"You think I look young?" He pulls the sheet over his naked groin. "How old do I look?"

"Old enough to be a dad." I pat my stomach. "When we get back to Manhattan we'll see that doctor Cleo recommended and we'll find out if we're having a daughter or a son."

"It's a boy." He leans forward to cup his hand over mine. "I know it's a boy."

I know that too. I'd seen a doctor here in Paris after I missed my period shortly after we arrived here. I knew before he told me that I was pregnant, that the baby had been conceived the night Dane left the airplane ticket on my pillow. I'd felt different when I woke up the next day and that feeling of pure joy and contentment had only gotten stronger after we'd moved here and decorated the small studio apartment the school had provided for us.

"It is a boy," I whisper as I look down at the gentle curve of my belly. I'm barely starting to show and unless someone knew that there was a life growing within me, they wouldn't guess that I was expecting a child with the man I love.

He moves even closer, resting his cheek against mine. "Did the doctor tell you that, Bridget?"

"No," I say honestly. "I feel it but I'll be so happy if it's a girl too."

Dane swallows hard and nods his head as he taps his chest. "Me too."

I stare at the tattoo on his chest. He's explained it's meaning several times but I've never asked him to translate what each word means. It's a German poem that his mother wrote for him and his brother when they were toddlers. I'll meet his brother when we get back to New York. Dane's insistence on getting him to attend our wedding paid off when Landon called to say he'd be there, all Dane had to do was name the time and place.

"Zoe will pick us up at the airport," I say quietly. I hate to leave this place. We only have one more week here before we have to head back to the lives we left behind.  My portraits had been so well received here that I've been granted a gallery showing of my own back in New York. I've started to garner the attention of art collectors across the globe and the biggest supporter through all of it has been Dane.

He cups my face in his hands. His right thumb brushes over my cheek. "I told my mother that I was going to marry you once we got back to New York."

"What did she say?"

"She was happy." A small smile takes over his mouth. "She told me she was happy for us."

I believe him. Anja has come to Paris twice since we've been here and although the first visit was filled with silent pauses and awkward glances, she'd taken the time to get to know me. She'd come to my first gallery showing here and had greeted my parents with a quick embrace and thoughtful words about how talented she thought I was.

By the time she flew across the ocean to see us again, Dane had told her about the baby. She was emotional, open and when she spoke about meeting her first grandchild there were tears in her eyes.

We may never be as close as she still is to Maisy, but we're making progress and the arrival of our baby in just under a half a year, will cement our bond more. I feel it.

"I don't want a big wedding," I repeat the same thing I've said almost daily since he proposed a month ago. "I don't need a ring either."

"I have a ring for you." He taps his bare chest. "I have vows for you too."

"What?"

"My mother gave me my father's ring after he died. It was his wedding band. I'm having a diamond put into that and they'll size it to fit this finger." He runs his index finger over my left hand. "It's at that jeweler we saw near the market. They do amazing work."

I'd sat on a bench, sipping a fruit juice while Dane had wandered into that shop last week. He'd emerged with a wide grin on his face and little to say. I knew that he'd gone inside to look at rings, but now, as I realize the meaning behind the ring I'll wear forever, I'm overcome with pure emotion.

"I started writing my vows to you when we got to Paris," he confesses. "I'm working on them but I already know the last line."

"Tell me what the last line is."

"My heart is yours. Keep it forever. Never let it go."

I reach forward to rest my hand over his against his bare chest and just as I lean in to kiss his mouth, I whisper the words back to him. "My heart is yours. Keep it forever. Never let it go."

# Preview of RISE

**A Three – Part Series**

"I know you, don't I?"

He doesn't. He's been watching me from across the room since he walked in right after the first model hit the catwalk. I expected all kinds of men to file through the door tonight. Even though I'd arranged for the premiere fashion show of the Liore lingerie brand to be held in an abandoned warehouse on the Lower East Side, I knew it would draw a specific, upscale, crowd.

One glance around the room and it's easy to spot the familiar celebrity faces, but hidden within the throngs of people who have gathered in this space, are friends of the company's owner and the competition, clearly visible beneath the mask of a grin and a small lie about being an acquaintance of one of the models.

I'd tossed the guest list aside when I saw the first media crew approaching the sliding metal door that leads into the space. I wanted the attention, and if it meant people who weren't invited drifted in to watch the parade of scantily clad women march up and down the makeshift stage that was constructed, hours ago, I'm on board. Gabriel Foster, the owner of the Liore boutiques, paid me well to get as many eyes as I could manage on his product, and I've done that, in spades.

"Excuse me." The stranger taps me on my forearm. "I think we've met."

I look up and into his face. It's handsome. It's so handsome that I'd remember meeting him, or even seeing him in passing on the street.

"I'm sorry," I say patiently. "I've very busy right now. I assure you that we've never met."

"You're 2B," he murmurs in a deep growl. "I remember you from the lavatory."

I'd moved to Manhattan six months ago after graduating from college. I've had my fair share of men hit on me, which says little about the way I look and more about the fact that single women in this city seem to be a rarity. I may have stood out in a crowd back in the small town I lived in on the outskirts of Boston, but here, in one of the most populous cities in the world, my long dark hair and green eyes don't set me apart from the crowd. I'm just another woman who doesn't sport a ring on her left hand which means I'm ripe for the attention of any man who is looking for someone to warm the other half of his bed.

I've grown accustomed to the expected requests to buy me a drink and within that there have been a few who have actually approached me with an intelligent conversation in their back pocket, but this one, this may be the one that I'll remember long after tonight.

"The lavatory?" I adjust my left heel, hoping that the movement will relieve the pressure I feel on the ball of my foot. I've been wearing these shoes all day and I'm ready to head home to kick them off so I can crawl into a warm tub.

"You were on a flight from Milan to JFK the week before last." His blue eyes rake over my black dress. "You were wearing a red skirt, white blouse and your hair was pulled back, tight, into a ponytail."

*What the fuck?*

I part my lips to say something, anything, but the dark haired, bearded stranger isn't done yet.

"You sat in business class, first class, actually on that flight. You were assigned seat 2B."

I was. I remember it clearly because I'd asked for that specific seat. It's the one I always request. I wouldn't say I'm a nervous flyer but if I can quiet my anxiety over being thousands of miles in the air in a confided space with dozens of strangers, I'll do it. That particular seat has always kept me safe so why mess with a good thing?

"You walked out of the lavatory. I was standing there, next to you and I remember the scent of your perfume." His hand reaches down. I don't protest as he gently grabs my wrist and brings it to his face. He inhales, slowly.

I look around the room, wanting to find a familiar face that will ground me in this moment. There's no way this is happening. I'd remember if this man sat next to me on a flight. I'd recall the curve of his strong jaw and the sound of his voice.

"I'm sorry. I don't remember," I admit.

"Allow me to introduce myself then." He slides his fingers up my wrist until his hand is cradling mine. "I'm Landon Beckett. Captain Landon Beckett."

"Captain?" I ask carefully, realization washing over me.

His full lips curve into a wry smile. "Yes. I was piloting the airplane."

My stomach knots. It's him. I thought I'd never see him again. There's no way he knows about the conversation I had with the woman sitting next to me. He can't know that, can he? "It's nice to meet you."

"It's my pleasure, Ms. Marlow or can I call you Tess?"

I take a step back as I feel a flush race over my body. "How do you know my name?"

"That's an interesting story." He crosses his arms over his chest. "Where do I begin?"

*Coming This Summer*

# Preview of HAZE

Featuring Gabriel Foster

"How long have you worked here?" His voice is cultured, deep and smooth. It's not uncommon to hear a voice like that in this boutique. I've worked here for six weeks now and at least twice a week a man with too much money and an insatiable need to see young women dressed in expensive lingerie will come waltzing through the doors.

"Welcome to Liore," I say softly as I glance to my left to where he's standing.

I have to look up. He's large, not just in height but in his shoulder's breadth. His eyes are a rich brown, his hair just as dark. His nose is sculptured and his jaw has a definite curve to it. The suit he's wearing is dark blue, perhaps even black. It's hard to tell under the chandelier lights that decorate this opulent space.

"Isla." His eyes hover over my chest before they settle on my name tag. "It's nice to meet you, Isla."

"It's lovely to meet you…" I pause. It's not only because I've been instructed to grab the name of each customer to give them a personal shopping experience. I want to know his name.

"Gabriel," he offers with a light touch of his hand on mine.

The name is oddly familiar. As I work to place it, I see him peering across the boutique at my boss. "Is there something I can help you find, Gabriel? Are you purchasing something for a girlfriend, or perhaps, your wife?"

His expression shifts slightly. "I have neither."

That's a pity but it's not. This is exactly the type of man I envisioned in my mind's eye when I arrived in Manhattan. I graduated from high school less than two years ago and my dreams of attending Julliard on a scholarship had vanished as quickly as my clean record when I broke one too many rules in high school.

"Is there something in particular that you're looking for?" I catch the faint wave of the hand of one of my co-workers across the aisle. I ignore it because when a customer is ready to buy, the store could be engulfed in flames, and I'm not moving an inch. The commissions here are the highest I've ever earned in retail and the secret to guarantee a big sale is to make the customer feel as though they're the only one in the boutique.

His eyes scan the various bras we have displayed before they move to the lace panties and garters. "If I asked you to try something on for me, Isla, would you do that? Would you take me into one of the change rooms with you?"

I've read the employee handbook. No, I skimmed it briefly while on my way to work that first day weeks ago. The number one rule is to never take a customer into the rooms. Men who lead you into those quiet spaces are craving more than a private fashion show. I know that. "I'm sorry, Gabriel. That's against company policy."

He studies my face carefully. The dark shadow around my blue eyes looks hideous in the alarming bright light of the morning, but in here it's sensual and alluring. My shoulder length blonde hair is straight today, a sharp contrast to my high cheekbones. I'm here to sell lingerie and the light pink wrap around dress I'm wearing accentuates everything it needs to. He hasn't walked away yet, so he's still primed to buy.

He closes the short distance between us as he steps towards me. "You don't strike me as the type of young woman who follows all the rules."

It's tempting. Not just because of the extra money I'd find in my pocket. "I don't follow rules, Gabriel. If you want a private show, I can come to your office after work."

His brow cocks with the suggestion. "Is that something you offer to customers often?"

I've never offered it before. "I only offer it to the ones who peak my interest."

"I'll give you my card." His hand dips into the inner pocket of his suit jacket.

I take it from his long, elegant fingers and look down at it. I don't have time to read the details before my boss is upon us.

I turn to look at her but she's staring at Gabriel. Her hand leaps to his shoulder.

"Mr. Foster," she says slowly. "I see that you've met our newest girl. Isla, you're explaining everything we offer to Mr. Foster, yes?"

I look down at the card of Mr. Gabriel Foster, the CEO of Foster Enterprises and the man who owns this boutique.

"Isla has been very cordial." He glides the tip of his index finger along my wrist. "She's coming by my office today. I'll expect you at four, Isla."

"At four," I repeat back. "I'll be there at four, Sir."

His eyes skim slowly over my body before they stop on my face. "Don't be late and bring those samples we spoke of."

I freeze as his hand runs up my arm before he brushes past me towards the front of the shop.

*Coming Soon*

# THANK YOU

Thank you for purchasing my book. I can't even begin to put to words what it means to me. If you enjoyed it, please remember to write a review for it. Let me know your thoughts! I want to keep my readers happy.

For more information on new series and standalones, please visit my website, www.deborahbladon.com. There are book trailers and other goodies to check out.

If you want to chat with me personally, please LIKE my page on Facebook. I love connecting with all of my readers because without you, none of this would be possible.
www.facebook.com/authordeborahbladon

Thank you, for everything.

# ABOUT THE AUTHOR

Deborah Bladon has never read a romance hero she didn't like. Her love for romance novels began when she was old enough to board the bus, library card in hand to check out the newest Harlequin paperbacks. She's a Canadian by heart, and by passport, but you can often spot her in New York City sipping a latte and looking for inspiration for her next story. Manhattan is definitely her second home.

She cherishes her family and believes that each day is a gift for writing, for reading, and for loving.

Made in the USA
Monee, IL
31 October 2019